Rob Beresford

And she had no intenti... ... ...
game.

Then he lifted his head and looked at her. No. More than that. He seemed to be studying her. She had been expecting those famous piercing cobalt blue eyes to give her the beauty parade head-to-toe assessment.

He didn't. His gaze was locked onto her face as though he was searching for something, and finding it. Because one corner of his mouth had turned up into just the hint of a smile, which only drew her attention to that kissable mouth.

'I think we've met before somewhere, but I am embarrassed to say that I've forgotten your name. Can you help?'

His voice was hot chocolate sauce on top of the best butterscotch ice cream and it had all the potential to make her silly girl heart spin just fast enough to make breathing a challenge.

Could she what? Oh, was that the best he could do?

'Oh, please. Does that line still work?'

Rob's eyebrow arched and a sexy smile designed to defrost frozen food at twenty paces was switched on like a lightbulb.

'Occasionally.'

Dear Reader

Since walking away from her high-flying job in the financial world Lottie Rosemount has been revelling in her new life as baker extraordinaire at Lottie's Cake Shop and Tea Rooms. It's set on a busy London high street and Lottie loves meeting the wide range of customers of all ages who have welcomed her into their community.

The one person she does not expect to run into is Rob Beresford, a gorgeous head chef who is just as notorious for his lack of social skills as for the award-winning recipes he creates for Beresford Hotels.

Five years earlier Rob almost brought her fledgling career crashing to the ground, but now her best friend is dating his brother. They *have* to get along!

Rob cannot commit to any girl for more than a few months. Lottie is looking for a long-term relationship. But perhaps Rob can persuade her to have just one tiny fling…with him.

I do hope that you enjoy travelling with Lottie and Rob on their journey to discover where they truly belong and who they belong with.

I love to hear from my readers, and you can get in touch by visiting www.ninaharrington.com

Nina

THE SECRET INGREDIENT

BY
NINA HARRINGTON

MILLS
BOON

Published in Great Britain 2014
by Mills & Boon, an imprint of Harlequin (UK) Limited,
Eton House, 18-24 Paradise Road, Richmond, Surrey, TW9 1SR

© 2014 Nina Harrington

ISBN: 978 0 263 91091 9

Printed and bound in Spain
by Blackprint CPI, Barcelona

Nina Harrington grew up in rural Northumberland, England, and decided at the age of eleven that she was going to be a librarian—because then she could read *all* of the books in the public library whenever she wanted! Since then she has been a shop assistant, community pharmacist, technical writer, university lecturer, volcano walker and industrial scientist, before taking a career break to realise her dream of being a fiction writer. When she is not creating stories which make her readers smile her hobbies are cooking, eating, enjoying good wine—and talking, for which she has had specialist training.

Other Modern Tempted™ titles by Nina Harrington:

TROUBLE ON HER DOORSTEP

CHAPTER ONE

ROB BERESFORD STEPPED OUT of the black stretch limo onto the red carpet outside London's newest and most prestigious art gallery, slowly rolled back his shoulders, and stretched out to his full height.

Rob ran the fingers of his right hand through his mane of collar-length dark wavy hair in a move he had perfected to draw attention to what, according to the Beresford hotel group marketing department, was his best feature.

'Make sure that your fans see that fantastic head and shoulders shot,' his agent, Sally, kept telling him. 'That's what your millions of lady followers will be looking for. Make the most of it while you can!'

Ah. The joys of self-promotion.

After twenty years in the hotel business Rob knew the drill inside out.

He gave the press what they wanted and they loved him for it. They had seen him on good and bad nights and both sides played the game when it suited them.

It was a pity that the paparazzi made more money when he was playing the bad-boy celebrity chef than on all of the other countless occasions when he was working in the kitchens creating the award-winning recipes for the Beresford hotel restaurants.

They wanted him to misbehave and throw a tantrum and

grab a camera. Punch someone out because of a careless re-
mark or lose his temper over an insult to his family or food.

The Rob Beresford they wanted to see was the young
chef who had become notorious after he physically lifted
the most famous restaurant critic in Chicago out of his chair
and threw him out of the Beresford hotel restaurant when
he dared to criticise the way his steak had been cooked.

And sometimes he was tired enough or bored enough to
let them goad him and provoke him into a stupid response,
which he instantly regretted.

Press the red button and watch the fireworks. Oh, yes!
But not tonight.

For once he was not here to celebrate the Beresford name
or promote his TV show or best-selling cookery books. Tonight was all about someone else's success. Not his. And
if that meant that he had to act out his part in public yet
again, then so be it.

He was wearing the costume; he had rehearsed his script.
Now it was time to act out his part until the star of the
show arrived.

Tonight he needed the crowd to love him and play up
the success of the art gallery. And the artist whose work
had been chosen to be exhibited for their prestigious grand
opening event. Adele Forrester. Fine Art Painter. And his
mother.

But inside his designer clothing? *Inside, he was a wreck.*

Even the photographers in the front row only a few feet
away could not see the prickle of sweat on his brow on this
cool June evening and he quickly covered up the tense-
ness in his mouth with a broad smile so that no one would
ever know that, for once, Rob Beresford was more than
just nervous.

He was dreading every second of the next few hours and
would only be able to relax when he was safe back in the

hotel room with his mother, congratulating her on a stunning exhibition that was bound to sell out fast.

The plan had been simple. They would arrive together, his mother would smile and wave a couple of times and Rob would escort her sedately into the exhibition to the sound of applause from her faithful fans and art lovers. Proud son. Star mother. Winner all the way.

So much for that plan.

The past week had been a blur of rushed last-minute arrangements and then a twenty-four-hour cold virus, which had been going the rounds in California, had knocked her out for most of the day. Followed by a serious attack of first-night nerves.

Until an hour ago he'd thought that he had succeeded and his mother was dressed, made up and ready to go, smiling and happy that after eight years of preparation her work was going to be shown in public.

But then she had made the mistake of peeking out of the hotel front entrance, seen the press pack and scurried back into the room, white-faced and breathing hard. Trying to control her panic while pretending that it was about time that she walked down the red carpet on her own. After all, this was her special night. No need to wait. She would make her own grand entrance. Why did she need her handsome son stealing her spotlight?

Right. She was forgetting that he knew her. Only too well.

So the limo had driven around the corner with him inside alone. While she cowered inside her hotel room, going through the relaxation exercises one more time. Afraid to come out and walk a few steps down a carpet and have her photo taken.

And just the thought that his beautiful mother did not

think she was ready or good enough for this crowd was enough to make his blood boil.

They had no idea how far she had come over the past few years to get to the point where she could even think about turning up in person to an exhibition of her paintings.

And they never would.

Fifteen years ago he had made his mother a promise.

He had given her his word that he would protect her and take care of her, and keep her secret, no matter what. And he had kept that promise and would go on keeping that promise, no matter how much it had impacted his life and the decisions that he had been forced to take to keep her safe.

He had stayed in Beresford hotels in cities close to the major psychiatric specialist units and turned down gigs in restaurants other chefs would kill to have worked in, just to make sure that his mother had a stable environment when she needed one.

Not that she liked cities. Far from it. He had lost count of the times he had made mad dashes to airports wearing his chef's clothes so that he could keep her company on a long flight to the latest new creative retreat that she had heard about, that afternoon. And suddenly it was the only thing she needed to complete her work and *she had to go that day or the rest of her life would be in ruins*.

No time to pack or organise anything. Then she was on her way, usually without the things she needed, but it had to be done now.

So he had to drop everything and go with her to keep her safe. Because when she was manic she was amazing, but there was one universal truth: whatever soared high had to come back down to earth. Fast. And hard. Sometimes very hard.

Walking down a red carpet and smiling was a small

price to pay for being able to support his mother financially and emotionally.

Rob scanned the rows of photographers lined up behind the mesh barriers on either side of the narrow entrance and acknowledged some of the familiar paparazzi that followed him from event to event whenever he was in London with a quick nod and a wave.

The rest of the pack jostled for position at the barricade, calling out his name, demanding pose after pose.

Fans held up signs with his name on them. Cameras flashed wildly. All desperate to capture a rare evening appearance from the chef who had just been shortlisted for Chef of the Year. Again.

Spotlights hit him from every angle.

He turned slowly from side to side in front of the floor-to-ceiling poster for the gala exhibition of new work from Adele Forrester, making sure that her official photograph and the poster would always be the background to any of his photos.

One hand plunged into his left trouser pocket. One hand raised towards the crowd. Wearing his trademark pristine white shirt and dark designer suit. No tie. That would be too conventional. A call to look this way then that was answered with a swagger. He rolled back his shoulders, lifted his chin and went to work the crowd.

It had taken him every day of the past ten years to create an image and a brand that served him and the Beresford family well and now was his chance to use it to help his mum.

A pretty brunette in her twenties held out one of his recipe books, stretching towards him, her stomach pressed against the metal barrier and shoulders so low that he had a perfect view down her deep V-necked top into a very generous cleavage.

Rob quickly stepped forwards, grin locked in place, his pen already in his hand, and signed a flourish of his name on the cover page while the crowd went mad behind her, screaming and calling out his name at ear-damaging volume.

He walked slowly down the line, signing yet another recipe book—one of his early ones—then a poster from his restaurant-makeover show.

And then the questions started. One male voice and then another.

'Is Adele turning up in person tonight for the show or has she done a runner like last time?'

'Where have you hidden your mum, Rob?'

'Have you left her behind in that treatment centre? Is that the only kind of artist retreat she knows these days?'

'Are the rumours true about her retiring after this show?'

Louder and louder, closer and closer, the questions came from every direction, more pointed and all demanding to know where his mother was.

They were goading him. Pushing him harder and harder, desperate for a reaction.

They wanted him to explode. To push the camera down someone's throat or, even better, give one of them a black eye.

A few years ago? He would have done it and taken the consequences. But tonight was not about him and he refused to let the press win, so he pretended to have developed sudden hearing loss and politely ignored them. This of course made them goad him even more.

Nine minutes later he had walked the whole of the line, smiling and laughing towards the waiting crowd, leaning in for the compulsory mobile phone shots.

Then just like that the press turned away as the next limo pulled up and, without waiting for permission or a good-behaviour pass, Rob turned his back on the crowd and photographers and strode purposefully down the last few feet of red carpet, through the open door of the art gallery and into the relative calm of the marble atrium where the other specially invited guests were already assembled.

This preview show was the one exclusive opportunity for the art critics to admire and study his mother's work without having to share the gallery with the general public. That was the good news. The less-good news was that it had been the art critics who had descended on his mother like a pack of rabid wolves when she had imploded at her last exhibition in Toronto.

Having a screaming and crying nervous breakdown in public was bad enough, but for her tormented and terrified face to be captured for ever by the press had made it worse.

Instead of defending her for her fragile creativity, they had condemned her for being a bad example to young artists for her excessive lifestyle.

But that was eight years ago.

Different world. Different faces. Different approach to mental illness. Surely?

Rob paused long enough to take a flute of chilled champagne from a passing waiter and was just about to launch into the media crew clustered around the gallery owner when he caught sight of his reflection in the installation light feature.

A sombre dark male face glared back at him, his heavy eyebrows low above narrowed eyes and a jaw that would be a better fit on a prizefighter rather than a patron of the arts.

Yikes! Maybe not.

He didn't want to terrify the critics before they had even had a chance to see the artwork. And most of them seemed to be enjoying the refreshments.

A quick scan of the room confirmed that unless there

was a back door through the kitchen, he was trapped. Unless... Yes! There was one person who was taking time to actually see the paintings instead of networking over the catalogues and free booze before the food was served.

A pretty blonde woman. Correction. Make that a very pretty blonde. She was sitting completely alone at the far end of the gallery, away from the hustle and noise from the street. Her gaze appeared to be completely engrossed in the artwork in front of her.

Rob turned away from the other guests, nodding to people as he passed, and started strolling down the gallery space, taking the time to scan some of the twenty-two paintings that he knew inside out.

He could give the critics a full history of each and every brush stroke. Where and when and what mood his mother had been in when she painted them. The hours spent debating locations and the quality of the light. Desperate for each work to be perfect. Flawless. Ideal.

The despair that came when they did not match up to her exacting standards.

The joy and delight and laughter of walking along beaches day after day, which only seemed to make the darker ones blacker. Like the time he was called out of a business meeting when she set six of his favourite canvases on fire on the hotel patio in a barbecue pit. That depression had lasted weeks.

These paintings truly were the survivors.

Especially the canvas that the blonde was looking at that very minute.

Rob exhaled long and slow. He should have known that a critic would be drawn to such a totally over-the-top sentimental and emotional piece.

It was good—no doubt about that.

But it was so obvious that his mother might as well be

standing there waving a banner telling the world that she had painted it in a dark time when the depression had almost become too much and she'd had to go back on the much-hated medication again.

It was probably the only piece that he had suggested to his mother to leave behind in her villa in Carmel, California. It was just too personal and way too deep to show to the world.

Too late. Because there it was. Not the biggest painting but the most intimate and revealing in the whole collection.

But just who was this woman who had obviously spotted the best picture in the room?

Rob stood to one side, sipping his champagne, and watched her for a few minutes in silence, his gaze scanning her pose, her body, her clothing, taking it all in and trying to make sense of what he was seeing.

She certainly didn't look like one of his mother's art critic pals or the hyenas back in Toronto. Failed artists every one of them. Far from it.

Straight blonde hair falling to her shoulders, she was wearing a sleeveless aqua dress and he could just make out a line of collarbone above a long, slender, elegant neck, surprisingly overlaid with muscle as opposed to starved thin like most fine artists he had met.

And she really was stunningly pretty. A break in the clouds outside the window shone a beam of sunlight onto the cream-coloured gallery wall, which reflected back from her skin. It became luminescent and pale. No artificial tan for this girl. She truly was all white peaches and cream.

But what were her hands like? At the moment they were pushed flat against the bench on either side of her body, palm down, but as he watched she lifted her shoulders and her hands clasped around her arms as though she was cold.

The air conditioning was certainly chilly but it was more than that. She was holding on to herself.

Totally wrapped up in her thoughts. Contained. Calm. Her gaze locked on to the painting as though it was the most important thing in the world. She was transfixed. Oblivious to the world. Totally caught up in the painting.

Because she got it. It was so obvious.

And for the first time that day—no, make that the first time this month—he felt that little bubble of a real smile pop in his chest.

Perhaps there was at least one art critic in the room to-night that was going to make him change his mind about their species?

Now all he had to do was find out her name and…

'Rob. So pleased that you could make it.' Rob blinked away his anxiety as the gallery owner came forward to shake his hand and, with one pat on his shoulder, guide him back towards the entrance to introduce him to several of the press who were clustered around the media table.

He glanced quickly over one shoulder back to the blonde, but she had turned slightly away from him to take a call on her mobile.

Later. He would find out a lot more about this woman… later.

Lottie Rosemount chuckled into the mouthpiece of her mo-bile phone. 'You really are shameless, Dee Flynn! But are you quite sure that Sean does not mind me using his hotel for the fundraiser? He is doing me a seriously big favour here.'

'No need to panic, oh, great organiser lady.' Dee's fa-miliar laughing voice crackled down the phone. 'Let's call it one of the many perks to having a boyfriend who just happens to run his own hotel chain. Sean expects you to invite the great and good of London town and fill his hotel to bursting. And once they see how fabulous his new hotel is? Job done.'

'Oh, is that what it is. A perk? Nothing to do with the fact that the lovely Sean would jog to the moon and back if you asked him. Oh, no. But I am grateful. You are a total star! Thanks, Dee. And have a great time in the tea gardens.'

'I will, but only if you stop worrying, missy. Yes, I can hear it in your voice. Just because a few hundred people will be turning up on Saturday night doesn't mean that you have to be nervous. They will hardly notice that Valencia has not turned up. You wait and see.' Then Dee's voice changed to a breathless gasp. 'Sorry, Lottie. They're calling my flight. Miss you, too. But we need the tea! Bye, Lottie. Bye.'

Lottie held the phone in her hand for a few seconds before clicking it closed and exhaling. Very slowly.

Worried? Of course she was worried. Or should that be terrified?

She would be a fool if she wasn't.

What if the fundraiser was a flop? There were so many creative people bursting with talent who needed a helping hand to get started living their dream. Scholarships to help gifted chefs find training was only the start. But a big start in more ways than one.

Pity that Dee had to be in China this week. She could have used some moral support.

Especially when the celebrity chef she had booked as the main attraction for the fundraiser had just cancelled that morning. It had taken months of pleading and cajoling before multi-award-winning chef Valencia Cagoni had finally agreed to turn up for the night.

Yes, of course Lottie understood that Valencia was still with her family in Turin because both of the four-year-old twins had chickenpox and were grounded as infectious tyrants. And no, Valencia was way too busy with the cala-mine lotion to think of another chef who could step in at such short notice and take her place.

Thank you, Valencia, my old boss and mentor. *Thanks a lot.*

Panic gripped her for a few seconds but Lottie willed it back down to a place where she kept all of the suppressed fear and suffocating anxiety that came with taking on such a huge responsibility.

This fundraiser had been her idea from the start, but if there was one good thing that her father had taught her it was that she always had options. All she had to do was think of one. Fast.

Lottie shuffled from side to side on the hard seat and tried to get a comfier position. She was going to have to give the gallery owner some feedback before his paying customers started complaining about having frozen bot-toms.

On the other hand, this was not a museum and she had been sitting in one place a lot longer than she had planned. Wealthy clients looking for artwork to adorn their walls would not be perched on the end of a leather bench for more than a few minutes while she had been sitting there for— Lottie checked her watch and snorted deep in the back of her throat in disbelief—twenty minutes.

Amazing.

This was the first time in weeks that she had been able to steal a few minutes to enjoy herself in between running her bakery and organising the fundraiser and she was quite determined to enjoy every second of it. Because she prob-ably would not find another slot before the event.

But she had always been the same. Every time her mother bought a new piece of art for one of her interior design clients, it was Lottie who had the first look before the piece was shipped off to some luxury second or third or, in one case, eighth home around the world. That was all part of her mum's high-end design business.

If Lottie saw something she liked she took the opportunity to appreciate it while she could. It was as simple as that.

Having the time to enjoy works of art was probably the only thing she really missed in her new life.

Of course she had known that running a cake shop and tea rooms would not be a nine-to-five job, but, *sheesh*, the hours she was working now were even longer than when she worked in banking.

She loved most of it. The bakery was her dream come true. But when her photographer friend Ian had casually mentioned that he was looking for a caterer to serve canapés and mini desserts for the opening of a new gallery specialising in contemporary art she had jumped at the chance.

Lottie's Cake Shop and Tea Rooms needed a photographer to take images for the bakery website and Ian needed food for the gallery tonight. Now that was the kind of trade she liked and it had nothing to do with her old job working the stock market.

Lottie glanced back at the main reception area.

She could hear the visitors start to arrive and gather in the bar area that had been opened up onto the stunning patio overlooking the south bank of the Thames on this cloudy June evening. The weather was warm with only a slight breeze. Perfect. Just the way she liked it.

Her skin did not do well in hot sunshine. Too fair. Too freckly.

Much better to stay here for a few minutes and enjoy this painting all to herself while she had the chance before the evening really got started.

The food was all ready to be served in the small kitchen behind the bar, the waiting staff would not be here for another ten minutes, and even the artist had not made an appearance yet.

So she could steal another few minutes of glorious self-indulgence before she had to go back to work.

This was her special time. To be alone with the art.

Lottie waggled some of the tension out of her shoulders and rolled her neck from side to side before lifting her chin and sighing in pleasure.

Most of the exhibition was high-art portraits and landscapes in oils and multimedia in a startling bright and vibrant colour palette, but for some reason she had been drawn to this far corner of the room. It was away from the entrance and the drinks table but was bright with natural light flooding in from the floor-to-ceiling windows.

And the one picture in the whole collection that was muted and subtle.

It was a small canvas in a wide red glass frame just like all of the others.

But this one was special. Different. She had seen it in the catalogue for the exhibition that her friend Ian had created and had been immediately drawn to it.

It was hard to explain but there was just something about the image that had taken hold of her and refused to let her go.

Lottie's gaze scanned the picture.

A middle-aged woman in a knee-length sleeveless red dress was standing on a sandy shore edged with pine trees and luxuriant Mediterranean plants. She was slender and holding out her arms towards the sea.

Lottie could almost feel the breeze in the chiffon layers that made up the skirt as they lifted out behind her.

The woman's head was held high and tall and there was a faint smile on her lips as she stared out to sea, reaching for it with both hands while her pale feet seemed totally encased in the sand.

It was dusk and on the horizon there were the characteristic red and gold and apricot streaks in the misty shadows that stretched out to the horizon. Soon darkness would fall but Lottie knew that this woman would stay there, entranced, until the last possible moment, yearning for the sea, until the very last of the day was gone.

While she still had a chance for happiness.

A single tear ran down Lottie's cheek and she sniffed several times before diving into her bag for a tissue, but then remembered that she had left them back at the cake shop, so made do with a spare paper napkin she had popped into her bag for spillages.

Last chances. Oh, yes. She knew all about those.

Until three years ago she had been a business clone in a suit, trapped in cubicle nation in the investment bank where her father had worked for thirty-five years. All she'd had to do was keep her head down, say the right things and do what she was told and she'd had a clear career path that would take her to the top. She'd even had the ideal boyfriend with the right credentials on paper just one step higher than her on the ladder.

How could her life have been more perfect?

The fact that she hated her job so much that she threw up most mornings was one of the reasons she was earning the big bucks. Wasn't it?

Until that one fateful day when all of the pretence and lies had been whipped away, leaving her bereft and alone. Standing on a beach like the one in the painting. Holding out her arms towards the sea, looking for a new direction and a new identity.

She wasn't balls-of-steel Charlie any longer, the girl who had walked away from her six-figure salary and the career track to the top of her father's investment bank to train as a pastry chef. Oh, no.

That girl was gone.

The girl sitting with tears in her eyes was Lottie the baker. The real girl with the real pain that she had thought she had worked through over these past three years but was still there. Catching her unawares at moments like this when the overwhelming emotion swallowed her down and drowned her.

For the first time in a long time she had allowed her public face to slip and reveal that she was hurting.

Foolish woman! Exhaustion and unspoken loneliness made her vulnerable. That was all.

The paper napkin was starting to disintegrate so she stuffed it back into her bag.

Maybe at the end of the night when everyone was heading home she could steal a few minutes with the artist and ask her about 'Last Chances'.

Who knew? Maybe Adele Forrester might be able to answer a few of her questions about how making the most of last chances could change your life so very much. And what to do when all of the people and friends that you thought would stick by you decided that you had nothing in common with them once you jumped ship and stopped answering your calls.

Starting with that, oh-so-perfect-on-paper boyfriend.

Yes, maybe Adele had a few answers of her own.

With one final sniff, Lottie blinked and wiped her cheek with the back of her finger. Time to repair the damage to this make-up and get ready to rock and roll. She had two hundred portions of canapés to plate out.

Busy, busy.

Yes, she should really make a move now. Oops. Too late.

Lottie sensed rather than heard someone stroll closer

and stand next to her, so that they were both looking at the canvas in silence for what felt like minutes but was probably only seconds.

'It's perfect, isn't it?' Lottie sniffed as yet another tear ran down her cheek, preventing her from turning around and embarrassing herself in front of a complete stranger.

'Absolutely perfect. How does she do it?' Lottie asked. 'How does Adele capture so much feeling in a flat image? It's incredible.'

'Talent. And a deep feeling for the place. Adele knows that beach at all times of day and season. Look at the way she blends the ocean and the sky. That can only come from seeing it happen over and over again.'

Lottie blinked again, but this time in surprise.

He understood. This man, because it was a man's voice and definitely a manly pair of designer trousers, was echoing the exact same thoughts that were going through her head.

How did he do that? The tremor in his voice was instantly calming and restorative. Someone else saw the same things in this work that she had. How was that possible?

It was unnerving that he knew what this painting was all about and could talk about it with such passion.

And then the harsh reality of where she was struck home and she felt like a fool. Ian had told her that this was a preview show for art critics and media people. This man was probably a friend of Adele Forrester who knew perfectly well the history behind the picture.

Maybe he could answer her question?

Lottie lifted her chin and shuffled sideways on the bench so that she could look up into the face of the man standing by her side.

The room froze.

It was as though everything around her slowed down

to treacle speed like a DVD or video being played in slow motion.

The laughter and gossip from the clusters of elegantly dressed people gathered around the gallery owner became a blur of distant sounds. Even the air between them felt colder and thicker as Lottie sucked in a low, calming breath.

Was this really happening?

'Rob Beresford,' she said out loud, and instantly clenched her teeth tight shut.

Thinking out loud had always been her worst habit and she'd thought she had it beaten. Apparently not. Her mouth gaped open in confusion.

And why not?

Rob Beresford. Her least-favourite chef in the world. And the man who had single-handedly tried to destroy her career.

CHAPTER TWO

'IN THE FLESH.' Rob shrugged. And without asking permission or forgiveness he sat down next to her on the flat leather-covered bench and stretched his long legs out towards the exhibition wall. 'I hope that you are enjoying the exhibition. This piece is really quite remarkable.'

Lottie tried to make her senses take it in. And failed.

Rob Beresford.

Of all the people in the entire world, he was the last person she expected to meet at a gallery preview show.

He looked like a picture postcard of the ideal celebrity chef. Stylish suit. Hair. Designer stubble. Damn the stylist who had his clothes pitched perfectly.

But underneath the slick exterior the old Rob was all still there.

She could see it in the way he walked. The swagger. The attitude and that arrogant lift of his head that made him look like a captain of some sailing ship, looking out over the ocean for pirate ships loaded with treasure.

He had not changed that much since their last meeting almost three years earlier.

When he had fired her from her very first catering job.

Just thinking about that day was enough for an ice cube large enough to sink the *Titanic* to form in the pit of her stomach.

She had only been working as an apprentice in the Beresford hotel kitchen for three months when the mighty Rob Beresford had burst into the kitchen and demanded that the idiot who had made the chocolate dessert go out into the dining room and apologise in person to the diner on his table who had almost broken his teeth on the rock-hard pastry he had just been served.

Apparently Rob had been totally humiliated and embarrassed. So he'd needed a scapegoat to blame for the screw-up.

In one glance the head pastry chef had nodded in her direction and the next thing she'd known Rob had grabbed the front of her chef's coat and used it to haul her up to his face so close that she could feel his hot, angry, brutal breath on her cheek. His anger and recrimination had been spat out in the words that would be burnt into her heart and her mind for the rest of her career.

'Get out of my kitchen and back to your finishing school, you pathetic excuse for a chef. You don't have what it takes to be in this business so leave now and save us all a lot of wasted time. Nobody humiliates me and gets away with it.'

Then he'd flung his hands back from her jacket so quickly that she had almost fallen and had had to grab hold of the steel workbench as Rob had stabbed the air. 'I don't want to see you here tomorrow. Got it?'

Oh, she'd got it, all right. She'd understood perfectly how unfair and how prejudiced these chefs were. She had waited until the sous chefs had stopped fawning at him and plated up new desserts before slipping out to grab her coat and escape from the back door before the pastry chef, skanky Debra, who had been so drunk that she could barely stand never mind make decent *pâté sucrée* that evening, could say another word.

From that moment she had vowed to be her own boss. No matter what.

Which begged the question…what was he doing here tonight? In an art gallery of all places? Buying art for the restaurants? That was possible, but not fine art. No, it was much more likely that there was someone in the room who could advance his career in some way.

See and be seen was Rob Beresford's motto. It always had been, and from what she had seen of him in the press and TV, nothing had changed. And if he had to pretend to have some knowledge of the pieces, well, that was a small price for his personal advancement.

The humiliating thing was he did not seem to have recognised her. She had been consigned to the box where all of the other sacked apprentices went to be forgotten. And she had absolutely no intention of reminding him.

Lottie ran one hand over the back of her neck to lift her hair away from her suddenly burning skin as a flash of anger shot through her.

Rob's powerful, low voice seemed to resonate inside her head and a whole flutter of butterflies came to life in her stomach.

His presence filled the space between them and she felt crowded out, squeezed between the ivory-painted wall and the bench. Last time he had towered over her, his eyes like burning lasers, and she refused to let that happen again.

Not going to happen. This time she was the one who glared at him face-to-face.

Hard angles defined his jawline and cheekbones but they only made the lushness of his full mouth even more pronounced.

At some point his nose had been broken, creating a definite twist just below the bridge. Thank heaven for that.

Otherwise this Rob Beresford had all the credentials

for being even more gorgeous than the last time that they had met.

As Rob reached for a champagne flute the fine fabric of his shirt stretched over the valleys and mounds of his chest muscles, which came from a lifetime of hard work rather than lifting weights in a city gym. There really was no justice—that a man who could create dishes as he could was good-looking, too.

Shame that he knew it.

In one smooth movement he pushed the sleeve of his designer dinner jacket farther up his left arm, revealing a curving, dark tattoo that ran up from his wrist. It seemed to match the design that peeked out in the deep V of the crisp white dinner shirt he was wearing unbuttoned. No tie.

For a tiny fraction of a second Lottie wondered what the rest of the design looked like on that powerful chest. Then she pushed the thought away. Body art on a chef? Oh, that made perfect sense…not.

Typical exhibitionist. Just one more way to draw attention to himself.

In the small world of high-level cooking it would be impossible not to run into Rob Beresford at the many chef award ceremonies where she was with the lesser mortals sitting in the back row.

And of course there was his TV show. It took guts to walk into a strange kitchen and tell the chef that the way they had been running their restaurant needed to be turned around and he had all the answers.

The TV audience could not get enough of the fireworks and tears and family trauma that came with having a complete stranger telling you how to run your life after years and years of working day and night. It had to be the third or fourth season. Why did these places apply? Madness. She certainly would never do it.

He was precisely the kind of man she had come to despise for the games that he liked to play with other people's lives. Pushing them around. Uncaring and selfish.

Harsh? Maybe. But true all the same.

What had she promised herself the day she walked out of the bank? No more lies. No more kidding yourself. No more second best. And no more putting up with other people's games.

Rob Beresford was a player.

And she had no intention of being part of his little game.

Then he lifted his head and looked at her. No. More than that. He seemed to be studying her. She had been expecting those famous piercing cobalt-blue eyes to give her the beauty-parade head-to-toe assessment.

He didn't. His gaze was locked on to her face as though he was searching for something, and finding it. Because one corner of his mouth turned up into just the hint of a smile, which only drew her attention to that kissable mouth.

'I think we have met before somewhere, but I am embarrassed to say that I have forgotten your name. Can you help?'

His voice was hot chocolate sauce on top of the best butterscotch ice cream and had all the potential to make her silly girl heart spin just fast enough to make breathing a challenge. More American than it used to be but that was hardly surprising. In fact, if anything, that trace of an accent only added to the allure.

Could she what? Oh, was that the best he could do? Try and make her feel guilty for causing him embarrassment?

She was almost insulted.

Surely the famous Rob Beresford had better pickup lines that that? Or perhaps he was not on top form. There was certainly something different about Rob. A little less arrogant, perhaps? Not surprising. He certainly got around, if you could believe the hotel and catering trade press.

'Oh, please. Does that line still work?'

Rob's eyebrow arched and a sexy smile designed to defrost frozen food at twenty paces switched on like a light bulb.

'Occasionally. But now I am even more intrigued. Put me out of my misery. Have we met before?'

'We might have.' She blinked and then casually turned back to face the canvases on the wall in front of her. 'But then again I didn't expect to find you in an art gallery. Have you changed direction? Or perhaps you want to meet a different type of girl? They do say that museums and galleries are very popular with single people these days. So tell me—how do you come to know Adele Forrester's work? You seem to be something of a fan. Am I right?'

She heard Rob take a short breath. 'I might be. But here is an idea. You seem to be very curious about me and I am curious about you. What if I answer one question then you have to answer mine? Simple trade. Question for question. What do you say? Do we have a deal?'

Lottie raised her eyebrows, then squinted at him. 'Can I trust you to keep your word?'

'Now I am offended,' he tutted. 'Absolutely. Just this once. And I promise not to ask any personal questions. Scout's honour.'

'You were never in the Boy Scouts!'

'Two weeks on the Isle of Wight getting sunburnt and learning to light fires. I remember it well. And you haven't answered my first question.'

Lottie could almost feel the prickle of interest build under her skin as his gaze stayed locked tight on her face.

Maybe she could take a few minutes to chat with him? Equal to equal? Pretend that they had never met? It would make a change from talking to Ian about the fundraiser and the photography shoot he was planning. It might even be amusing to see him struggle to recall where and when they last met.

'Okay,' she casually replied as though she didn't care either way.

'Okay? Is that it?'

'That is all you are going to get from me, so take it or leave it,' Lottie replied with a small shoulder shrug. 'And I get to go first. My question. Remember?'

'Right. Yes, I know Adele Forrester and, yes, I am a huge fan of her work. Love everything that she has ever exhibited and a lot more besides. Happy now? Good. Because now it is my turn to ask for the name of my inquisitor. Because whatever paper you are working for has certainly chosen the perfect character for their entertainment section. So. What name shall I look out for in the Forrester review?'

Lottie nibbled on the inside of her lip to stop herself from smiling. Ah. So he thought she was one of the art critics. *Perfect. She was officially incognito. This was going to be fun.*

'Charlotte. But you can call me Charlie. I answer to both.'

'Charlie,' he repeated in a low voice, then blinked twice before shaking his head from side to side. 'An art critic called Charlie. I should have known it would be something like that.'

His trademark collar-length hair swung loosely in front of his face as he moved, then he flicked his head back out of habit rather than design and a low rough chuckle rumbled deep in his throat before he laughed it away.

'Thank you. I needed that. And does Charlie come with a surname?'

Patience. There was no way that she was going to allow

this arrogant man to win his little game. Her surname would instantly give the game away.

'You are so impatient. That is a completely new question. It's my turn now.'

Lottie tilted her head towards the canvas and pushed her lips together. She had met enough art critics through her mum to give a decent enough performance for a few minutes.

'This is such an interesting piece. But it seems so different from the other paintings in the exhibition. Most of the landscapes are luxuriant, and the portraits jump off the page—they are terrific. But this one is more…'

Lottie waved her hand in the air as she tried to come up with the perfect description and failed.

'Introspective?' Rob whispered. 'Was that the word you were looking for? The colours capture Adele's mood. Every artist has shades to their work and their character. The dark makes the light seem brighter. Don't you find?' And with that he turned and gave her a smile that had nothing to do with teeth and everything to do with the warmth of genuine feeling that illuminated his face, from the gentle turn of those full lips to the slight crease in the corner of each eye.

After years working in the hard world of banking where a wrong call could cost millions, Lottie prided herself on being a good judge of character.

And this version of Rob Beresford threw her.

He meant it. He was so…calm and centred…and normal. At that moment he was simply a man in an art gallery having a conversation about an artist that he sincerely admired.

Where had that come from?

Was it possible that he had changed so much in the past few years?

'Would you call yourself an artist, Rob? The media certainly seem to think so.'

His eyes widened and just like that the tiny thread of connection that had been linking them together on this slim bench snapped with a loud twang and went spinning off into the room.

'Charlie! Every chef would like to think that they create art on a plate. Colours, tastes and textures. But an artist? No.'

With a quick toss of his head he raised his eyebrows. 'You surprise me, Charlie. Surely you don't believe everything you read in the press? I would hate to be a disappointment.'

'Ah. I knew there was a reason why I never wanted to go down the celebrity route. The price of fame. It must be so exhausting. Having to act out the part every time you show yourself in public when all you want to do is stay home and watch reality TV shows in your pyjamas with a cup of hot chocolate.'

'Drat. You have found one of my private fantasies.'

And then Rob paused and leant a little closer. *Too close.* Blocking her view of the rest of the room but forcing her to focus on just how full his lips were and how the dark hair on his throat curled into the open neck of his crisp white shirt.

He lifted his right hand and stroked the line of her jaw from ear to throat with the pad of a soft forefinger, his touch so light that Lottie might almost have imagined it.

But that would have been a lie because the second his skin met her face Lottie sucked in a sharp quick breath and her lips parted, revealing in the most humiliating way possible that she was not immune to his touch.

Just the opposite. She knew that her neck was already flaming red in a blush that engrossed her.

Which was more than humiliating; it was a bad joke. Rob Beresford's reputation with women was common knowledge in the catering world and the Beresford hotel kitchens had been alive with gossip about who he had seduced and then dumped in quick succession. She had seen it herself.

One single quiver of sexual attraction was not going to change her mind about him. It was biology and a much underused libido playing tricks on her.

Her gaze scanned his face.

At this distance she could see that his eyes were not just blue, but a blend of different shades of blue from steel-grey to the bright evening sky. Mesmerising. Totally, totally mesmerising. And quite shameless.

Because before she had time to protest, Rob cupped the nape of her neck with one hand and bent his head lower so that his nose was pressed against her forehead, his breath hot and slow and heavy on her face.

Without asking for permission she felt his other hand fan out on her lower back, taking her weight, arching her body down. Into his control.

His lips trembled and parted. *He was going to kiss her.*

Instinctively she slid her tongue across her parched lips but instantly saw his smile switch back on.

Damn. She had fallen straight into his little trap.

'What are you doing?' she breathed and raised both hands to push his away. 'You are being outrageous. Don't you ever go off duty? Please don't try and flirt with me, Mr Beresford.'

'There we go. Another one of those damn fantasies of mine.'

Rob pushed both hands down hard, slid off the bench and stretched to his full height so that when he spoke he had to look down at her with a huge grin on his face. 'After all, I would hate for you to think that I was acting out of character for some reason. That might be too much for your readers to understand. Because otherwise, who knows? It might actually cross your mind that I am simply here to enjoy the art on my night off.'

His gaze locked on to her eyes and held them tight in its grasp. Only now those blue eyes were more gunmetal than warm sea. Laser cold. Sharp. A cold shiver that had nothing to do with the icy air conditioning raised goosebumps along Lottie's arms and neck.

So this was what it was like to be at the receiving end of one of Rob Beresford's bad moods.

Not good. *So* not good.

The cold shiver turned to fiery indignation and Lottie pressed her lips together. What gave him the right to talk to a guest at an art gallery like this?

One more minute and she was going to jump up and give him just as much right back, starting with the last time they met. Maybe he could dish it out but could he take it when the tables were turned and he was on the receiving end? She doubted it.

Lottie curled her fingers into a tight fist and mentally came up with a couple of suitable put-downs from her banking days, but she never got the chance to use them. Because just like that he broke eye contact and rolled back his shoulders for a second before looking back over one shoulder at her.

'I've just had an outrageous idea. Plus it's my turn for a question. Care to join me on a tour of the exhibition? It's about time you gave me your expert opinion on the other paintings.'

Rob ran one hand back through his hair and tore his gaze away from the blonde and looked around the room. A trickle of guests was starting to wander into the exhibition space now and he inwardly cursed himself for being stupid enough to lose his temper and act out his frustration with this girl he had just met.

He was so tired of playing the fool for the cameras. Tired of allowing his emotions and excitement to get the better of him.

Just once it would be nice to be taken seriously.

He was Adele Forrester's only child. Did the press, like this cute blonde, really think that he had no appreciation of the art world after spending most of his precious free time in the company of a woman who was even more obsessed and passionate than he was?

'You want to hear my opinion of the other paintings, Mr Beresford? Is that right?'

He flicked his head towards the reception area. 'Absolutely. I think I just saw some waiting staff coming in. Why don't we find out what culinary delights the gallery have lined up for us this evening before the rest of your colleagues arrive? You never know. Some of them might even be edible! Oh—and, Charlie, tonight you can forget the Beresford. Right here, at this moment, I'm just Rob. Think you can handle that? Or are you scared of living dangerously?'

He offered her his hand and she lowered her head and stared at it, flicked her gaze onto his face, then back.

'Danger is my middle name. I think I can just about manage that. Rob.'

But just as she stood up her head bobbed to one side and she saw someone behind his back. 'Oops. Duty calls. I would love to stand around and feed your ego a little longer but I have to get back to work. Another time, perhaps. Have a lovely evening. Ciao.'

And with a tiny finger wave of her right hand she strolled—no, she sashayed across the room on four-inch heels as though she were made to wear them, giving him the most excellent view of the sweetest clinging dress above spectacular legs.

She had a waist he could wrap his hands around and meet in the middle, and the way she lifted her chin as she strode away?

Dynamite.

This girl moved as if she were gliding. Head held high and still, focused on the path ahead, determined. She was like a swan on the water, a perfect example of restrained elegance, both understated and explosively seductive.

Even the way she walked screamed out that she came from a background of old money plus an expensive education and all that came with it.

Either that or she was the best actor that he had ever met, and he had met plenty of actresses in the hotel and restaurant trade. Hollywood and Broadway. A class and C class. They were all the same under the slick exterior. Girls ready and waiting to say the words someone else had written for them.

But Charlie the art critic? Charlie was in a class of her own.

And in his crazy world, that was pretty unique.

Who was this woman and what had he done to upset her? He had met her before, that was certain. And from that frosty glare she had given him when he'd sat down next to her, chances were that it had not been one of his finer moments.

Now all he had to do was work out what terrible crime he had committed. Rob could never resist a challenge.

He was going to chase this woman down to her lair and find out her name before the night was out.

Maybe he could salvage something out of his nightmare of an exhibition after all?

'Charlie. Just a moment,' he said to her back, and strode after her across the exhibition space, back towards the re-

ception area where waiting staff were stacking side plates
and cutlery onto white tablecloths over polymer tables.

It had been a long day and his body clock was starting to
kick in. Perhaps it was time to show his appreciation for the
lady who had finally given him something to smile about?

With his long athletic legs and her shorter high-heeled
ones, it only took Rob a few steps to catch up with Charlie,
who surprised him by stepping behind the desk.

'Hold up. You never did give me your name. A business
card. Email address. Phone number, if you are old school.
Come on. You know you want to keep in touch. For...fol-
low-up questions.'

Rob's voice faded away as he stepped closer.

'You're wearing an apron. Are you waiting tables?'

'You're right, the rumours about you could not possibly
be true. You *are* more intelligent than you look,' Charlie
said, and flashed him a glance in between giving directions to the very young-looking art-student waiters. 'But
I can only hope that you have a sense of humour, as well.
Because it's even worse than that. You see, I am not an art
critic. Never have been. Probably never will be. I'm the chef
who is taking care of the canapés this evening.'

And before Rob had a chance to take it all in, Lottie
picked up a tray of steaming-hot savouries and thrust it out
towards him like a weapon.

'Could I interest you in one of my humble pies? I think
they are just what you need.'

CHAPTER THREE

'NOT AT THE MOMENT, THANK YOU. No. I think I'll pass.'

Rob picked up one of the business cards that Lottie had fanned out next to the condiments and the deep frown creased his forehead as he read the address out loud.

'Lottie Rosemount's Cake Shop and Tea Rooms? That's where Dee Flynn works.'

Lottie could practically see the cogs of Rob's mind work as his gaze ratcheted up one notch at a time from the business card past the platter of savoury canapés and finally to her face. Where it settled for one millisecond as the inevitable hit home.

'Please tell me that you're not Lottie Rosemount.' He finally groaned.

Her breath caught in the back of her throat for a second before she smiled it away with a quick flick of the head.

Busted! Playtime had officially just ended and it was back to work.

'Sorry. Can't do that. Life is so unfair sometimes. Don't you think? Welcome to my world, Mr Beresford.'

Shame. She had enjoyed being taken seriously as an art expert for a few minutes. Now it was back to being plain old Lottie the cake maker. It was always curious to see how people's expectations changed when she announced that she baked for a living, but she had not expected to see that stunned look on Rob's face. He was in the same business, after all.

Her body still tingled at the touch of his hand at the small of her back. One thin layer of silk was all that had separated his clever long fingers from her naked skin.

Time to jump in and take control while he was still at the glaring-in-disbelief stage. 'I did tell you that my name was Charlotte and people call me so many nicknames that it's fun to have a change now and then. Just for the variety.'

'Lottie Rosemount.' Rob nodded slowly up and down, then gave a low whistle. 'I don't believe it. So you like playing games with people? Lottie. Or do you have another nickname you prefer to use on social occasions?'

Games. *Hell, no.* He was not accusing her of playing tricks on him.

'Oh, no. Lottie works fine. As for playing games? On the contrary. It goes against my principles.'

His reply was a choked cough and he gestured towards the bench, which was already occupied by other patrons.

'But it was okay to string me along just now and pretend that you were an art critic. Did you even like that painting you were staring at or just doing it to impress me?'

She heard the annoyance in his voice and was shamefully delighted.

'I don't recall saying that I was a critic. And as for trying to impress you? Well, someone has a very high opinion of themselves. For the record I have always adored contemporary art and I love these pieces. Especially that painting. If that is okay with you? Or are you one of those people who think that the catering staff should stay in their place? Out of sight. So that they are not able to embarrass the management.'

His back stiffened and instantly Rob seemed to grow about five inches taller.

'No. I am not one of those people, Lottie. Far from it, actually.'

The words whirled around inside her head at the confused signals. He was acting as if she had insulted him. Well, that was rich.

'Good. Because I do love that painting and was pleased to have the chance to see it. So, seeing as we share a common interest, I think it only fair that I share my other passion with you before the masses of starving media arrive.'

'You have more than one passion? Please, carry on. I would hate for you to feel that you cannot act on your principles. *Heaven forfend.*'

Ignoring the sarcasm was not something Lottie found easy, but she got through it by focusing on opening up a new batch of bakery boxes.

The next thing Rob knew he was holding a dessert plate with a piece of cake on it. He lifted it to his nose and sniffed.

'Lemon sponge?'

'I do hope that you enjoy it. The gallery gave me strict instructions that Adele Forrester had specifically requested two desserts. Individual dark chocolate tarts and lemon drizzle cakes. A special order from a fine artist. Now that, Mr Beresford, I could not fake. Dig in.'

His lips closed around the forkful of cake and her gaze locked on to those lips.

She had never seen such sensual lips on any man before and, oh, boy, they looked good enough to eat. The tip of his tongue flicked out tantalisingly and wiped away a smear of lemon sauce.

A flash of raw and unadulterated attraction hit her hard. Unexpected and entirely inappropriate. Strange how it felt seriously good.

Do that again. Please.

Lottie didn't realise that she had stopped breathing until

a very loud ringtone smashed through her foodie trance and she instantly whipped the other cakes onto the platters and arranged them artistically on the buffet table so that the guests could help themselves.

Saved by the bell.

Rob put down his plate and casually fished the mobile phone out of his pocket, checked the caller identity. And flicked the phone closed with a crisp clip.

'Interesting cake. But I have to go and meet another lovely lady. I'll be seeing you around.' He smiled at Lottie, then gave her an outrageously over-the-top wink. 'You can bet on it.'

See you around?

Of course Rob was going to see her around.

His half-brother, Sean Beresford, was totally in love with her best friend and business partner, Dee, and unless she had totally misread the signs, there would be engagement parties and wedding planning before the end of the year. And right there next to Sean would be his best pal, Rob.

She was going to have to put up with Rob for Dee's sake. But really? Trying to flirt with her in an art gallery? Sheesh. And why did he have to be so...so...him?

So who was this lovely lady anyway? Some A-list celebrity? Or that supermodel Dee had told her he was seeing?

Lottie casually turned her head so that she could see Rob's back.

He was making a beeline for the tall, elegant, very slender older woman who was walking on air through the doors leading into the gallery. One hand was high in the air, the other waving from side to side from the wrist in flamboyant over-the-top gestures.

The moment she saw Rob she gave a quick squeal, flung her arms forward and gave him such a warm and sweet hug that Lottie knew that they cared about one another. He seemed perfectly happy to hook her arm over his and escort her into the room, lighting their way with the kind of beaming smile that should be licensed to power companies.

But it was only when she stepped closer under the exhibition spotlights that Lottie realised she was looking at Adele Forrester. She recognised the characteristic high cheekbones and profile from the posters and exhibition catalogues that her friend Ian had created.

And it totally floored her.

Adele was lovely, happy, laughing and enjoying herself.

Well, that was one more illusion shattered! So much for the tortured artist who had painted that wonderful landscape of the woman on the shore looking for a last chance. She had clearly found her mojo because right at that moment Adele Forrester was the star of the show, Rob Beresford was her escort and they were both having a great time.

Rob Beresford and Adele Forrester.

This evening was certainly turning out to be full of surprises. Little wonder that he was a walking expert on the artist's work when they were clearly such great pals. Not lovers. She could see that. No. There was none of that awkward first touch. They seemed closer. Almost like best friends or family.

Curious. She had not expected that. Perhaps she should call Dee and find out if Sean had mentioned anything about how Rob knew an artist like Adele Forrester.

Instantly the gallery owner and several of the guests surged forwards to shake Adele's hand, smiling and laughing and crowding in to get attention from the star of the show.

Lottie tried to peer over their heads but it was no good. Adele was swamped.

And right on time the first batch of art-student waiting

staff emerged from the kitchen carrying platters of hot canapés straight from the oven.

It was show time!

He had known that this was going to happen.

Worse. It was entirely his own fault.

He should never have left his mum alone at the hotel with the champagne that the gallery had sent around and several packs of cold medicine.

He had taken his eyes off the ball and indulged in a little free time with a lovely blonde who had turned out to be the opposite of what he'd expected.

And now his lovely mother was as high as a kite.

Flying over everyone's heads but coming down to earth just long enough to make polite and quite sensible conversation with the very people who had the power to make her life miserable if she imploded.

He had let her down.

There was no other way of describing it. The most important exhibition of her career and Adele Forrester had just described her signature style to the art critic of the largest broadsheet newspaper in London as Californian rain.

The real problem was that she adored chatting about her art so much. This was her world and she was amazing. Truly. Grabbing her arm and dragging her away would not only be creepy, but annoying.

That wouldn't work. So he had switched to plan B. The oldest technique in the world. Distraction and diversion.

Now. How many lovely lady art critics could he charm just long enough for them not to notice that the artist they had come to chat to was totally sozzled? *Time to find out.*

'Lemon drizzle cake! Oh, how did you know that was my absolute favourite? You are a complete genius and I don't even know your name. How embarrassing. My son never makes me lemon drizzle, no matter how often I plead with him.'

Lottie grinned and loaded a plate with three squares of moist cake. 'Lottie Rosemount. And I am told that your agent made a special request, Miss Forrester.'

'Oh, one more reason why I love Sally so much. And please call me Adele.'

Lottie watched Adele dive into her bag and sneeze onto a lovely hand-embroidered hankie, which was now sodden. She squeezed her eyes together, then blinked a couple of times.

'Can you believe it? I wait eight years for an exhibition and I have to come down with a horrible head cold. Almost through it, but my head! It feels as though it is totally full of cotton wool. Excuse me, darling. Time for another of these cold tablets I bought this morning. They really are the perfect pick-me-up.'

Adele popped one into her mouth and washed it down with a huge slug of pink champagne before smacking her lips. 'Quite delicious.'

Lottie took a quick glance at the medicine box Adele had left on the table.

'Er. Adele, those are one-a-day tablets. Are you sure it's okay to take so many with alcohol?'

'One a day? Really? Oh. Well, that must mean that they work faster. Excellent.'

Adele rested a beautifully manicured hand on Lottie's arm and swayed slightly. 'As long as they get me through the night, sweetie, I am prepared to take the risk. I have waited a long time for tonight. There is no way that I am going to miss a single moment.'

Then her eyebrows lifted and a huge sweet grin illuminated the room. 'Ah. There's my son. Better load my plate up with those delicious-looking bites before he catches up with me and reminds me that it is way past my bedtime.'

Then Adele flashed a completely over-the-top dramatic wink before blinking in rapid succession.

'A girl can always use more pizza squares. Don't you think? Ah. Rob. Perfect timing as always. Give your old mum a hand and hold my glass while I sample these pastries, will you, kiddo? They all look *so* good.'

Lottie inhaled a long slow breath, redolent with the aroma of the last of the mushroom-and-anchovy croustade slices Adele was tucking into with great relish, before slowly sliding her gaze up Adele's arm into the face of Rob Beresford.

The man who had sat down on that bench and let her prattle on about the paintings without even giving one tiny hint about why he knew so much about Adele Forrester.

Because apparently this lovely woman with the amazing artistic talent...

Was his mother.

There were bad words to describe men like Rob. And *kiddo* was not one of them.

And he had been accusing her of playing games!

Oh, Adele. Where had it all gone wrong?

The snake waited until Adele was chatting to Ian before sliding closer to the serving area. 'Charlie... No. I mean, Lottie. Good. You are still here.'

Rob glanced from side to side before asking in a low whisper, 'I need a back way out of the gallery and I need it fast. Start talking.'

His fingers started tapping out a beat on the table and his whole body language screamed out impatience and frustration.

Lottie glanced over his shoulder at the cluster of giggling press ladies in regulation black who had their heads pressed together comparing their mobile-phone photos and shoot-ing very unsubtle smoochy glances in his direction. Hair flicking and quick-fire reapplication of lip gloss seemed to be the order of the day.

'So I see,' Lottie replied with the same fixed, profes-sional smile that she had used all evening, the one that made her jaw ache. 'The owner has a very useful gallery plan. You will find it just over there. Behind the barman's head.'

Lottie pointed to the large display on the wall next to the drinks table, which was slowly emptying as the remaining guests wandered out onto the terrace to enjoy the cool late-evening air before heading home.

'What's the matter, Rob? Need to make your escape be-fore the girls pounce on you?'

The smile dropped from the handsome man's face and he half turned and flashed her the withering, contemptuous look that had made him notorious in the hard-nosed cook-ery shows, but had no place at all in a fine-art exhibition.

It was nothing like as angry as the look he had given her when he had fired her but Lottie reared back and pretended to dodge to one side. 'Oh, my. Are those daggers aimed at me? I do hope that the wind won't change because you would not want your face to stick like that.'

Then she leant forwards a little and winked. 'I worked in banking for many years. So the hard approach is wasted on me. Same goes for sighing loudly and frowning. Been there, done that. Not putting up with it a moment longer.'

Rob's eyebrows shot up and he stared at her in what looked like real astonishment.

To her delight the hard line of his mouth lifted up into the tiniest of smiles. 'Okay. Let's try it your way,' he re-plied in a low, hoarse voice that almost trembled with sup-pressed energy. 'Excuse me, Miss Rosemount, but could you please direct me to the back way out of the gallery through the kitchens?'

Her hands got busy stacking her bakery platters into a wide plastic crate. 'Of course, Mr Beresford. If you go through those two swing doors and walk about ten metres past the dishwasher there is a fire door to the main staircase to the building. It comes out at the loading bay at the back of the gallery.'

His reply was a quick 'thanks' as he strolled past her at jogging speed, one hand in his pocket as though he were boarding a yacht.

'You're welcome,' she murmured to his back.

What was that all about?

Or rather *who* was that all about?

Lottie swung the final platter and table cover into the carry crate and looked up to scan the room.

He certainly did not want to see someone here this evening. But who? Most of the critics had left when the food ran out and Adele had been around the gallery at least ten times over the last two hours, explaining each and every piece to them before returning to the bar for a refill.

Perhaps he had seen a former girlfriend he did not want to be photographed with? Or maybe one of the rival chefs on the bake-off contest had turned up and was itching for extra publicity.

There must be someone. Then a flash of blue sparkle just in front of one of the largest paintings caught her attention, followed by a peal of very loud and very over-the-top female laughter.

And Lottie's heart sank.

Because suddenly the reason for Rob Beresford's desire to explore other exits from the gallery became startling clear.

It was Adele Forrester.

And she had just staggered into one of the major installations from a very famous artist. It was by pure chance that the gallery owner had caught it in time to prevent a major disaster. On their opening night.

Ouch.

The problem was that Adele was treating it as a huge joke. Her hands were waving in the air but as she stepped forwards it was only too obvious that she was way too unsteady on her feet to be standing up.

Oh, Adele! Cold tablets plus champagne were a bad combination.

Any minute now she was going to fall over and embarrass and humiliate herself, which was the very last thing she needed!

Yep. *Back door.*

In a second she whipped off her apron and dropped it into the crate.

'Adele.' Lottie smiled as she strolled as casually as she could manage up to the stunningly dressed woman who was clinging on to the slightly intoxicated and more-than-slightly terrified gallery owner.

Adele turned towards her a little too quickly and her legs gave a definite wobble but Lottie stepped forwards, hooked her arm around Adele's, and took her weight before anyone had a chance to notice. 'I feel so guilty. I promised to save you some of that lemon drizzle cake you loved so much and now there are only three pieces left.' Then she grinned and snuggled closer as though they were the best of pals and intent on a girl huddle. 'I have kept them hidden in the kitchen for you. If you are ready?'

With one final laugh in the direction of the very relieved gallery owner, Adele clung on to Lottie and chatted merrily about how much she loved London. And cake. And champagne. But somehow Lottie held Adele mostly upright as they very slowly and sedately crossed the gallery and with one push they were through the doors and into the kitchen.

One bar stool and a plastic cake box later, Lottie could finally catch her breath and rub some life back into her arm. Give it five minutes and they would be on their way.

The sound of heavy male footsteps taking the stairs two at a time echoed up and Lottie closed her eyes.

Rob burst into the kitchen, his gaze taking in the scene, eyes flashing, dark and powerful. Accusing and angry. Full of that same fire and mistrust as the last time that they had met.

'What's going on?' he asked, and he jerked his chin higher with every word.

'Adele needs some air and lemon drizzle cake. I was helping her to get both. Okay?'

The Rob she had met three years ago had been obscenely confident of who he was. Master of the universe. Demanding and expecting everyone to worship his talent and magnificence. And that man was right here in the room all over again.

'I can take it from here. She's fine. Just fine.'

But as she nodded Lottie was incapable of dragging her gaze from those stunning eyes.

And the longer she looked, the more she recognised something so startling and surprising that it unnerved her.

Rob might appear to be the most confident and put-together and in-control man that she had ever met, but in those eyes she recognised anxiety and concern.

Something was worrying him. Something she did not know about.

'Have you organised some transport?' Lottie whispered, trying to sound casual so that Adele would not be scared.

'Don't worry about that,' Rob snapped. 'The most important thing is to get her out of here before she makes a fool of herself.'

Lottie smiled down at the lovely woman who was half leaning against the dishwasher and nibbling delicately at the cake, apparently oblivious to their conversation.

'Why? This is her party. Her work. Surely she is allowed to have fun at the opening night?'

'Not in front of these people. They are looking for any excuse to pull us down and sell the photographs to the highest bidder. They know me. And they know where to find me. The last thing I need is a scene. Not good at all.'

'*You.* They know *you.*'

Lottie stared at him open-mouthed and then shook her head in disbelief. 'Oh, I have been so stupid. I actually thought that you were concerned that your mum might embarrass herself on her big night. When all of the time you were more concerned about how this might look to the press pack waiting outside the front entrance. You and your precious image are the only things that matters.'

'You don't know what you are talking about,' he whispered, and she saw something hard and painful in those dark and flashing eyes.

'Oh, don't I? You would be surprised. I know a lot more about men who put their so-called appearance above everything else than you think.'

She could feel her neck flushing red but there was nothing she could do to stop it.

How many times had her father used the same expression? The last thing he wanted was a scene. How often had she stood next to him at company functions afraid to speak or even move, because he had given her strict instructions to stay silent and keep in the background? Don't make a fuss. You are an embarrassment. No one likes a show-off.

And never, ever, do anything that would put him in a bad light.

The one time she got drunk after a multimillion-dollar client signed with her and she arrived home in the middle of her parents' bridge party, happy and loud and laughing, her mother was so disgusted that she asked her to go to her room and stay out of sight in case her guests saw her.

No mention about her happiness. It had all revolved about her father's carefully stage-managed and totally fake image. Everything her family did was to make sure that the rest of the world never saw a crack in the carefully constructed outside persona.

He had been a tyrant, a bully and a liar. And a con man.

And now Rob was acting in exactly the same way.

She felt so angry with him she could hit him. The egotistical creep. Her fingernails pressed into her palms as she fought the urge to throw open the kitchen door and leave Rob to sort this mess out on his own.

'This is really good cake. Is there any more?'

Adele!

Guilt and shame shot through Lottie so fast that it blasted away her contempt for Rob and left her with a lovely lady who needed help.

In a click the fog that was clouding Lottie's brain cleared. It was Adele that mattered here, not Rob.

'Absolutely,' Lottie replied. 'In fact I am on the way to the bakery right now. Would you like a lift? I can drop you off at the hotel later if you like? When you're feeling a little steadier.'

'Great idea,' Adele replied and tried to pick up one of the wine glasses draining in the dishwasher tray. 'Oh. My glass is empty.'

'No problem. I have lots of lovely coffee and tea back at the bakery. And then when you get back to the hotel, your son here—' and at this point she flashed him a narrow-eyed squint '—can make you some lovely hot chocolate. How about that?'

Adele staggered to her feet and held out her arm. 'Lead the way. Cake ahoy.'

'I'm coming with you.'

'No can do. This is a two-woman delivery van. And Adele is quite happy in the passenger seat.'

Rob grunted and waved back to his mother, who was sitting quite sedately in the van with her seat belt already fastened, looking vacantly and very glassy-eyed down the lane behind the gallery.

In the end Lottie had given way and skipped ahead with her bakery crate while Rob had helped his mum negotiate the quite steep staircase to the delivery bay.

'Then drive to the hotel and I'll follow in a black cab.'

Lottie took a calming breath and then lifted her chin and leant closer to Rob so that she could talk to him through clenched teeth. 'And watch Adele fall out of the van onto her face in front of the cameras? Oh, that would be a good idea. Not a chance. Your mother needs somewhere to go for a couple of hours to rest and recover before she heads back to the hotel.'

Her hand flipped up. 'Dee is away in China and I have a spare room your mum can use if she likes. Next question.'

He stepped up so that their chests were almost touching.

'My mother is my responsibility. Not yours.'

Lottie narrowed her eyes and stared up at Rob. His face was in shadow from the street lights and security lamps, making the hard planes of his cheekbones appear even more pronounced.

'Let me make something very clear. I am not doing this for you. I am doing it for Adele. Bully.'

'Let me make something clear. I am not letting her out of my sight. Kidnapper.'

They stood there, locked in a silent stand-off as the air between them positively crackled with the electricity that sparked in the narrow gap.

And into that gap drifted a completely obvious but daring idea.

She needed a replacement chef for Valencia Cagoni at the charity fundraiser and Rob needed transport in her van. Maybe there was a way they could both get what they wanted?

Lottie inhaled a long slow breath through her nose as the plan took shape.

'There might be one way you could persuade me to let you travel in the back with my bakery trays. If you can lower your pride, of course. I realise that would mean coming down in the world from the kind of transport that you are accustomed to.'

A thunderous look and a lightning-sharp glare were joined by a hand-on-hip move that would no doubt terrorise any lesser female. But Lottie held her ground as he slowly walked around to the back of her white delivery van and peered inside.

'The back of the van?'

She nodded slowly up and down. Just once. 'There is a charity fundraiser on Saturday evening at the catering college we both went to. You were notorious. I was a star. The big-name chef who was lined up to attend can't make it. So I have to find a second-best alternative. I suppose you would do as a last-minute stand-in. Or do you want to go home in a taxi?'

His nose twitched. Ah. Perhaps there was still a faint sense of humour lurking there behind the scowl.

'One evening. Charity fundraiser. That's it.'

'Absolutely.' She grinned. 'Leap in.'

CHAPTER FOUR

'WELL, THE WAY SEAN TELLS IT, Rob was squeezed into the back of your delivery van all the way back to the bakery and you took every corner at speed just to make sure that he would be tossed around in the back as much as possible.' Dee giggled down the phone. 'Shame on you, Lottie Rosemount. Although…I would have liked to have been there to see it.'

'I don't know what you mean,' Lottie replied, with the phone jammed tight between her shoulder and her ear. 'A good dry-cleaner should be able to get the stains out of his trousers. Although chocolate and double cream sticky smears can be tricky, especially on cashmere.'

'You should try getting soy sauce out of a silk top!' Dee laughed and Lottie could visualise her friend wiping her eyes before sniffing. 'Now here is the thing, sweetie. I haven't told Sean that Rob was the head chef who fired you from your job when you were an apprentice. Secret squirrel, just like you asked. So the boy wonder is still in the dark at why his devilish charm is being wasted on you. At the moment. But you know how much chefs love to gossip and the fundraiser is at a Beresford hotel. Rob is bound to find out one way or another. So-o-o…it might be time to fess up and call it equals before the big night.'

'Equals? Oh, no. Rob Beresford doesn't get away that

easily. A twenty-minute van ride through central London does not match up to being fired from your dream job for something you did not do. I think I can stretch the retribution out for a little bit longer.' Then Lottie put down her mixing spoon and took the phone in one hand before asking in a low voice, 'Does that make me a bad person? Because I don't want him to turn me into an evil witch.'

'True. That coven look is so last year. But don't worry. You just want to make the boy suffer as payment for the horrible mistake he made when he let you go. His loss. I understand that perfectly. You have to get it out of your system and this is your chance to do it. And maybe have a little fun in the process. Am I right? And now I am going to be late. Email. Later. Bye.'

Lottie put down the telephone and thought back to that moment when she had turned around to find Rob Beresford sitting within striking distance of her and fun was not the first thing that came into her mind.

The sound of laughter rang out from inside the tea rooms and Lottie looked up as one of their regular gentlemen customers held open the door for two elderly ladies whose hands were full of shopping bags and the three cake boxes containing all they needed for a spectacular sixth birthday party for a very special grandson.

Her regular crowd of early shoppers were still enjoying the special-offer breakfast special. Cheese and ham panini followed by a freshly baked and still-warm blueberry and cinnamon muffin washed down with as much tea as they could drink. Good tea, of course. Dee Flynn might not be spending much time in the tea rooms these days but she made sure that the tea was as good as ever.

Sunlight flooded into the cake shop from the London street and bounced back from the cream-and-pastel-coloured walls.

This was how she had imagined it. Years ago when she was working the corporate life and popping into coffee shops for a triple espresso and a paper sack full of carbohydrates, fats and sugar just to get through the morning.

Her bakery. Her cake shop and tea rooms.

It was all real. She had done it. No, correction. She had not done this all on her own.

Lottie smiled and reached out for a spatula but then let her hand drop onto the worktop.

She missed Dee more than she would ever admit. Dee had been the one and only person she had asked to join her and it had been such fun planning the cake shop and tea rooms together. A girl who had a passion for baking and an Irish girl whose idea of heaven was the contents of the wonderful mystery packages that used to arrive from tea gardens all over the world.

But then Dee had fallen for Sean Beresford and now her life was one huge adventure. Exciting and thrilling. Her tea import company would go live by the end of the year and she was loved by a man who was almost good enough for her.

One day soon Dee would be off for good, leaving her alone. Again.

A woman's voice lifted up from the chatter and Lottie looked up in time to see a handsome couple in business suits laughing together as they strolled hand in hand down the pavement, a cake box swinging from the man's arm like an expensive briefcase.

From the side view the blonde in the designer suit and high heels looked so much like the old version of herself that Lottie clasped hold of the workbench for support.

Not so many years ago she had been that girl. Hardworking and driven, but happy to eat out in fine restaurants several times a week with the man her father thought was suitable boyfriend material.

Strange. She had taken it for granted at the time that one day she would move to the next step and marry the young executive, take the standard maternity leave and create a pristine and perfectly run home of her own with her two perfectly mannered children around her. One boy. One girl. All part of the grand master plan her parents had slotted her into.

The problem was she had bought into the whole family thing from the start and she still wanted it. Only this time the family she wanted was going to be very different from the one she had grown up in. That was not negotiable.

Cold, icy silences at torturous formal mealtimes would be replaced by warm, real interest in what the people around the unpolished practical pine kitchen table were thinking and doing. Helpful and supportive. Wanting the best for her children and being there for them no matter what happened and what choices they made. Working with a man who she could love as a real partner for the long haul.

A man who did not insist that every surface in the house was sanitised and polished daily in silent obedience by the slaves of women who were his token wife and daughter.

So, overall the precise opposite of what she had grown up in and survived.

Yeah. Well, that was the dream.

And her life at that moment was the reality.

No boyfriend. No family. No children of her own. And no prospects for creating that family unless something changed in her life or she made it happen.

When was the last time she had shared a meal cooked by someone else with a man who she could call her boyfriend—or even a lover?

When was the last time she had even gone on a date?

Lottie stood on tiptoe to watch the young executive couple press their heads together, happy and oblivious to how blessed they were, before they turned the corner and moved out of sight.

Drat Dee for showing her just what she was missing in her life.

One day she would find someone who she could trust enough to share her life and dreams with. One day.

When the phone began to ring again, Lottie had to take a moment to blink away stupid tears before picking it up.

'Lottie's Cake Shop and Tea Rooms.'

'Good morning, Miss Rosemount. I trust that you slept well.'

It was Rob!

Her foolish girly heart skipped a beat and her stomach flipped so hard that she had to grab the mixing bowl of icing before it slithered off the worktop.

Sleep? How did he expect her to sleep? It had taken hours to settle a very bouncy and over-stimulated Adele into Dee's room and persuade her not to munch the entire contents of the biscuit displays. Followed by several hours of tossing and turning as she replayed the scenes with Rob on repeat inside her head.

Breathe. All she had to do was breathe normally. Keep it casual. That was the key. Lottie's mouth curved up into a smile. He was totally in her control, and that felt disgracefully good.

'Splendidly, thank you,' she lied. 'Good morning to you, too. I hope that the bruises have faded?'

'Not yet,' a low rough voice replied. 'Those packing crates were lethal.' Then he gave a low cough. 'I was wondering if my mother was awake yet. We had agreed to catch up about her plans for the day.'

Ah. So that was why he had phoned. He was worried about how his mother was.

Okay. She got that. As long as Rob remembered that *she* was the person who had invited his mother to stay in Dee's room overnight, for the simple reason that she liked Adele Forrester and the poor woman was in no fit state to face the press.

And definitely *not* because her son Rob had looked desperate.

'As of ten minutes ago your mum was snuggled under Dee's duvet and snoring lightly. That cold medicine and champagne combination make a very effective knock-out potion. It may be a while before she surfaces.'

'Fine. See you in an hour. Try and get her up in time. *Ciao.*'

And then he put the phone down on her. *Unbelievable!*

Lottie glared at the handset in disbelief for a few seconds before shaking her head and returning it to the wall bracket.

That man had no manners whatsoever.

Lottie sniffed and picked up her spatula and got back to work filling an icing bag with the luscious soft-cheese-and-orange-zest icing for the mini carrot cakes that were already lined up in their cases and waiting for a soft swirl of Lottie's special recipe topping.

The cheek of the man. Just because he was a celebrity chef with his own TV show and food awards up to his armpits did not mean that he could simply order her about and expect her to say, 'Yes, chef,' like one of his kitchen brigade!

Lottie tossed the spatula back into the bowl and squeezed the piping bag down until she had formed a perfect swirl in the bowl.

But at least one good thing had come out of it all. Robert Beresford, international chef and gossip-columnist golden boy, had promised to turn up for the fundraiser at the hotel. And she was going to hold him to that, no matter what happened.

'Oh, can I lick the bowl out? Please? You know I cannot resist your icing! Mmm, delish.'

Lottie chuckled as her friend and part-time waitress wiped her fingertip around the scrapes of icing left in the glass mixing bowl and popped it into the mouth. 'Oh, that is *so* good,' Gloria moaned. 'When are you going to give me the recipe, woman? My girls would love me for ever.'

Lottie threw her head back and laughed out loud. 'What are you talking about, Gloria? Your three girls already think you're a goddess because you work here and go home loaded with edible swag every afternoon. And what about that handsome husband of yours? How did the chocolate melting-middle brownies go down last night?'

'Go down? Oh, yes. I am going to need a regular supply, if that boy has the stamina to keep up with me,' Gloria replied with a waggle of her eyebrows.

Lottie glanced quickly at the tables, then leant across and wiped the icing from Gloria's cheek. 'You are terrible! And setting a bad example for the customers.'

Then she flicked her head towards the counter. 'How are we doing out there? Ready for the carrot cakes?'

'Girl, we are always ready for that carrot cake. Pass them over and turn the oven on to make the next batch. They'll be gone in an hour. And before I forget, the gals have been asking me about the Bake and Bitch club meeting next week. What special treat do you have lined up?'

Lottie winked and started washing up. 'Wait and see, Gloria. You are just going to have to wait and see.'

Rob stared out of the floor-to-ceiling office window at the overcast sunless skies of central London in June. It was hard to believe that only thirty-six hours earlier he had been eating barbecue in the glorious Californian sunshine with his restaurant brigade.

His eyes felt heavy, gritty, and ready to close, but just as Rob rolled back his shoulders his talent agent, Sally Richards, finished the call on her mobile phone.

'Good news. The first reviews and photos of the exhibition are all looking brilliant. The only photographs I have seen are when she left the hotel for the event last evening. Adele smiled sweetly on the way out and gave them a lovely wave before jumping into the limo. Not a word about her staggering home early the worse for wear. So relax, Rob. You got away with it.'

'By the skin of my teeth and through the back door. What a nightmare,' he replied and then covered a yawn with one hand.

'So are you ready to rock and roll? Because I have to tell you, I have a tube of under-eye concealer in my bag and you need it more than I do. Did you get any sleep at all on the flight? Eight hours, wasn't it? Nine?'

Rob snorted a reply to the one talent manager he had used since he first stepped out from his dad's Beresford hotel chain and started making a name for himself.

'That was the New York leg of the journey. I had to stop en route from California to check up on a few things at the Beresford New York office. Then the traffic was horrendous. So I missed my flight to London and had to battle with the usual airport media scrum. So all in all just about a typical day's travel in the crazy world I live in.'

'Hey. That's why you love it so much!'

Rob looked around and blinked at Sally a few times before collapsing down on the leather sofa with a grin. 'If you say so, but these past few months have been a nightmare, Sally. My mum…well, you know my mum. Hates medics.

Always has done. She promised me that she would start taking the medication as soon as she finished the final piece for this exhibition, but I don't know. I called her from the airport yesterday and she sounded high as a kite. But last night she was so doped up with cold medicine it was hard to know what was going on inside her head.'

Rob ran his hand back and forth over his mouth and chin. 'It's been eight years since her meltdown at the last exhibition. Eight years, Sally! And the press are still baying for something juicy to say. I thought that if I came here I could provide some sort of diversion. You know what they're like. Why bother with a clever artist with a fading reputation when she has a TV celebrity as a son? Who knows? If we goad him enough we might be able to set off some of those fireworks and get some photographs to sell to the highest bidder. And they have the perfect ammunition to do it with.'

Sally walked around and perched on the edge of the desk.

'Did you manage to keep it together?'

There was something in Sally's tone that made Rob sit back on the sofa and look up. 'Barely. I would not give them the satisfaction. So don't give me that look. I played nice and did not punch anyone, no matter how much I wanted to. Happy? Because I know that voice. There's something else going on here. Fire away. Let's get it over with.'

'Observant as ever.' She smiled and paused long enough to reach across the desk and pass a bundle of printed sheets across to Rob, who glanced at them once before tossing them onto the sofa cushion.

'You cannot be serious. I've just finished filming the final TV series and it practically killed me fitting everything in. I've done the interviews and press calls and earned that money. And now they want me to do another series? What is that all about? We've been down this road before,

Sally. Mum needs me to be close at hand. Travelling across the States then flying back to get her through this exhibition has been tough on both of us. She needs me to be in California. And I really need to get back to work in the Beresford kitchens. Sean has hardly seen me this year and I have been relying way too much on the chefs I trained. Time to get back to doing what I do best. Working with food and creating amazing dishes for the Beresford hotel chain.'

Sally raised both hands in the air. 'I did what you asked me to. I made it clear to the production company a year ago that you have had enough of the restaurant makeover show for TV. One more series and that's it. But the audience figures are soaring higher month on month, Rob. Viewers cannot get enough of you. Look at the numbers, Rob. This is crazy money. Sign the new contract and you don't need to work again unless you want to. Ever. This could be just the opportunity you need to build up that emergency fund.'

Rob paused, then glanced up at the woman who had looked after his interests since he was seventeen. 'Come on, Sally. You know this was never about the money. Every penny I have earned on the TV shows and personal appearances has gone into my mum's account.'

'And last time I checked, the investment plan we worked on was doing very nicely and bringing in a respectable income to cover her not-so-little spending sprees. But how long is that going to last? You are top news at the moment. But once you move back into your kitchen the focus will shift onto the next hot new chef and Rob Beresford will not be the man of the moment any longer. And you can stop glaring at me. Because I'm not the only person who has got their head about that fact. So far I have had three enquiries from documentary film companies. Every one of them wants the exclusive rights to a behind-the-scenes exposé of the real Rob Beresford. And if you don't take part they will make them anyway. That's the way it goes.'

There were a few seconds of silence before Rob responded in a low voice. 'Are you telling me that someone else is planning to write my life story without even asking me?'

'Absolutely. That's why you should think about it. Because you know what would happen if they did. They are bound to focus on the one thing we've worked hard to keep in the background.'

Rob pushed himself shakily to his feet and walked stiffly over to the window, his shoulders rigid with stress. 'My mother would not survive. It took her months to pull back from the last bout of depression and I can't force her to take the medication while she is painting. It has to be her choice. That was what we agreed.'

'Then tell the story the way you want to before somebody else does.'

'Tell my story? You think the readers would want to know about all of the gruelling years I spent in hotel kitchens? There is nothing exciting and glamorous about that way of life.'

Rob rolled back his shoulders and winced. 'Speaking of which, I have an appointment with a baker and something tells me that I had better not be late.'

Sally coughed low in her throat and looked at him over the top of her spectacles. 'A baker? Today? I thought you would be spending time at the gallery with Adele.'

'I'll explain later, Sally...if I survive.'

It was mid-morning before Rob pushed open the door to Lottie's Cake Shop and Tea Rooms and stepped inside.

And almost whirled around on one heel and went straight back out again.

Because he had just walked into what looked like a children's tea party, complete with ear-damaging levels of laughing, calling out and crying, some sort of jangling music, and a group of toddlers swaying their bodies from side to side and waving their hands in the air just in front of the serving counter while the girl he now knew to be Lottie Rosemount was conducting the dancing with a large wooden spoon.

She was wearing wide-leg navy trousers and a floral T-shirt covered with a large navy apron with a picture of a cupcake on it. Her blonde hair was tied back in a high ponytail and a pretty navy-and-white headband drew attention to an oval face that even without a trace of make-up still managed to be stunningly pretty.

This was the place that Sean's girlfriend, Dee, loved so much?

He had survived restaurant opening nights that were quieter and more in control than this!

After a ninety-hour week and several international flights the last thing he wanted to do was join in a school party. His job was to earn the money so that his mother never had to worry about having nothing in the bank ever again.

But when could he ever refuse her anything?

She was the one and only woman on the planet who he had promised to take care of for as long as she needed him.

And he kept his promises. Even if that meant turning up to a small high-street bakery on a weekday morning.

'Thank you, ladies and gentlemen,' Lottie called out. 'That was simply amazing. Disco dancing and sporting stars of the future. No doubt about it. And don't forget, the Yummy Mummy club meets at the same time next week. So if you are ready to say the word about the one thing we all love best in the whole world…wait for it, Helena, and please stop doing that, Adam…three…two…one. Let's have a great big…*cake*!'

Rob winced and half closed one eye as the wannabe dance troupe screamed out the word and then they all burst into a barrage of yelling and screaming and calling and jumping up and down.

All he could do was stand to one side as the actually very yummy mummies wrestled their little darlings into submission and baby buggies and in some cases reins and shuffled past him towards the entrance and the busy London street outside on the pavement.

Holding the door open for them seemed like a good idea. The first time.

Except that the second each lovely mummy spotted him smiling politely at them the forward movement onto the pavement slowed down to the point where a very rowdy and disorderly queue had formed in the cake shop.

'Hello, handsome. Has anyone ever told you that you look a bit like that horrible rude chef that shouts a lot on the telly?' The second girl shrugged. 'Only not as good-looking. Sort off.' Then she covered her hand with her mouth and laughed before shuffling off.

'I get that a lot. No problem,' Rob called after her with a quick wave before helping a very attractive brunette with her buggy. His reward was a beaming smile and a small business card popped into his shirt pocket with a cheeky wink while the little girl in the buggy amused herself by painting the jam from her donut onto the leg of his trousers.

Charming.

Five minutes later he had to physically unwrap the fingers of one charming cherub from his jacket and slide backwards into the cake shop. In an instant he closed the door tight behind him, his back flat against the glass, and exhaled slowly.

'It must be nice to be so popular.' A familiar female voice chuckled and Rob opened his eyes to see Lottie staring at him from behind the counter. 'Are you available next Thursday morning? I'm thinking of doing Zumba for the under-fives. You would be a great hit for the lovely mums.'

'Sorry. Previous booking. And please tell me that it's not always like that.'

'Oh, no,' Lottie tutted. 'Sometimes it can be quite rowdy.' Then she smiled. 'But brilliant fun for the kids. They have the best time and the mums have a chance to meet their pals. I love it.' Then she pressed her lips together. 'Do you drink tea?'

'Don't tell Dee but I would love a coffee,' Rob replied and stepped forwards to the counter.

Lottie pushed her lips out. 'Let me guess. Double-shot Americano. The breakfast of champions.'

Just for one split second Rob thought about calling her bluff but just the thought of that coffee was making his mouth water.

'Damn. I hate to be predictable. Hit me.'

'With pleasure,' she whispered and then shook her head, rolled her eyes skywards and turned back to face him with a small shoulder shrug. 'House rule. If you are a guest you have to eat something baked on the premises with your beverage. The donuts lasted thirty seconds but I have grown-up cakes galore.'

Then she turned away and continued talking but he couldn't hear a word above the hiss and explosive steam from the coffee machine.

'Sorry, I didn't catch that,' Rob said and strolled casually around the counter and stepped up to Lottie as she tapped out the coffee grounds.

In front of him was a kitchen about the same size as the one in his London penthouse apartment, except this kitchen was jam-packed with stainless-steel appliances and what looked like two commercial-size ovens. The air was filled with the most delicious aroma of baked goods. Spices and vanilla combined with the unique tang of caramel and buttery pastry and fresh-baked bread. Rob took a moment to appreciate the aroma.

'What do you think you are doing?' she muttered between clenched teeth and whirled around and pressed both hands flat against his chest and pushed hard.

'Nobody—and I mean nobody—comes into my kitchen without asking me first. Do you let strangers just walk into your kitchen? No. I didn't think so. Step back. All the way. And stay there. Thank you, that's better. Take a seat and I'll be right with you.'

Then she exhaled slowly and stepped back to the coffee machine, mumbling under her breath as she went.

'Apologies,' Rob said and raised both hands in the air. 'My fault entirely. I am so used to walking into other people's kitchens I forgot my manners.'

'Um, well, I hope that you remember at the fundraiser,' Lottie replied and stabbed the coffee spoon in his direction. 'The whole idea is to raise funds for scholarships to the catering college. Not scare the VIPs away.'

'Hey. I can play nice when the occasion demands,' Rob replied and hit her with his sweetest smile.

'That's good to know.' Lottie sighed as she strolled towards his table carrying a tray with two steaming cups of coffee that smelt so good his mouth was practically watering before he sat down.

She took a breath, put the tray onto the table, and then shuffled onto the chair facing him.

Watching him take that long, deep sip of piping-hot black coffee. Just the way he liked it. Perfect.

'Great coffee. And thank you again for helping my

mother out last night. It was very generous of you,' Rob added with a slight bow of the head. 'I appreciate it.'

'No problem. Adele has been no trouble at all.'

Ah. Adele had been no trouble? So why did she think he would be?

With a low growl Rob put down the coffee and folded his arms and sat back in his chair so that he could face Lottie. 'You don't have a very high opinion of me, do you? Help me to understand.'

She blinked a couple of times and swallowed a long sip of coffee before her gaze flicked up into Rob's face and their eyes met. 'You were right, last night in the gallery. We have met before. About three years ago I was one of the catering students who had won a place in the Beresford hotel kitchens right here in London. You were entertaining guests one night and came in to see us after the meal and…you fired me. Gave me the sack. Threw me to the wolves. Let me go.'

Lottie clasped her hands so tightly around the coffee cup that Rob could see the whites of her knuckles and there was just enough of a tremble in her voice to make the hairs on the back of his neck prickle to attention. 'Remember the pastry chef? Debra? The one who could barely stand up that night, never mind create something amazing? Debra was the one who had made the desserts. But I was the one who got the blame and the sack instead of her.'

Lottie paused and then lifted her chin, defiance blasting out from those green eyes with all of the heat of a fiery dragon. 'It was no secret that you were sleeping with Debra at the time so you were not going to fire the person responsible for that particular disaster, were you? So I went. And she stayed. Does that help to make things a little clearer, Rob?'

CHAPTER FIVE

EVERY SOUND IN THE CAKE SHOP seemed to fade into the background as Rob focused on the bitter words that had exploded from the lips of the pretty girl sitting so still across the small table from him.

Of course he remembered Debra.

A shiver of cold regret and bitter disappointment bubbled up.

His rules were simple and easy to remember.

They could have fun. They could have a fling and a great time together and while it lasted he would be the most attentive and faithful boyfriend that a girl could want. Then they would walk away and get on with their lives.

That was how it worked and he made damn sure that any girl he dated was very clear that he was not in the business of negotiating. They were either in or out. Black or white. Their choice.

Debra had lasted longer than most and they had enjoyed a pretty good relationship for a few months. Until the inevitable had happened. She had started pushing for a long-term commitment that he hadn't been prepared to give. She had kept telling him how much she loved him and how different she was from all of the other girls, so his rules did not apply to her. She was too special and different to be treated like one of the others.

She had not felt so special when he'd packed his bags and had been out of her door an hour later. In fact he recalled crying, screaming, and a humiliating display of begging.

It was weeks later that he'd found out through the gossip channels that Debra had been getting over his breaking up with her with the help of vodka and free hotel wine.

Lottie was the apprentice pastry chef who he fired that night to teach Debra a lesson and try and shock her into taking her life back.

Well, that explained a lot.

'I remember it well. I ended up taking Debra home to her parents a few days later and finding her the professional help that she needed. It was a great relationship while it lasted and Debra is a remarkable girl. I met up with her and her husband when they were in Los Angeles for a professional chef conference last autumn. They seem like a great couple who have a stunning restaurant together. I am happy for her.'

Rob slowly unfolded his arms and stretched them out across the table.

'That was a long time ago, Lottie. I made a choice. It was the right decision at the time and I have to stand by that. End of story.'

There was a gasp from across the table and Lottie stared at him, wide-eyed.

'The right decision at the time? For who? Your squeeze?'

She sat back heavily in the chair and blinked. 'Is that it? Is that the only apology you have for me? Because I have to tell you that, as excuses go, that is pathetic.'

'No excuses. It was my job to recruit top talent for the restaurant and Debra is a great pastry chef. I didn't know about her drinking problems until they impacted her work.'

Rob leant forwards from the waist and pressed the flat of his hand down on the pale wood tabletop.

'My only regret is that I allowed personal feelings to block my judgement. I should have spotted that Debra was in trouble weeks earlier and done something about it before things got out of hand. Instead I stayed away to give her some distance. The last thing she needed was me standing looking over her shoulder and shouting orders at her. That was my mistake.'

'What about firing me as some sort of scapegoat? I was incredibly lucky to find another placement the next day after some serious pleading.'

A smile crept over his lips and he tilted his head towards Lottie. 'Sometimes I'm just too sensitive and caring for my own good.'

'Really? I had no idea.' Lottie nodded but every word was dripping with venom. 'You hide it so very well.'

'On the contrary.' Rob shrugged. 'Take this charity fundraiser you conned me into.' His hand flipped up into a question before he reached for his coffee. 'I cannot wait to hear all about it. For a start, I would like to know who's running the show. Whose idea was it to create scholarship funds for trainee chefs? Because I hope that they know what they're getting themselves into. That is one hell of a lot of hard work.'

The blonde sitting opposite leant forwards, her forearms on the table until her face was only a few inches away from Rob's nose, and smiled sweetly. 'That's an easy question to answer. It was my idea. I know precisely what I have got myself into and, yes, it is a lot of hard work. And I wouldn't have it any other way.'

Then she slid back, lifted her chin and smiled before replying. 'This time I am the one who gets to set the rules and call the shots. And I can't tell you how liberating that is.'

Then she nodded towards the plate she had slid towards

him. 'Take now, for example. No coffee without something to eat. This time it happens to be my speciality pear-and-almond tart. Enjoy.'

Rob stared at the food, and then looked up into a pair of sparkling green eyes.

Only Lottie's eyes were not simply green. They were forest green. Spring-bud green. The kind of captivating green that knocked the breath out of his lungs.

It was hot outside, but it had suddenly become a lot hotter in this cake shop.

It must be the heat from the ovens.

Her attention was totally focused on him, and her head tilted slightly to one side as she waited patiently for his reply for a few moments.

Just for a second, her gaze faltered and a chink appeared in the façade through which he got a faint glimmer of something unexpected. Suspicion, maybe, but a fierce intelligence and power. It lasted only an instant. But it sent him reeling, before the closed-mouth smile switched back on.

Lottie polished a pristine fork on a clean corner of her apron before placing it next to the pastry on Rob's plate. 'You know how hard it is to make a name for yourself in the catering world. I was lucky and so were you. We had money and backup. A full scholarship is the only way most of these young people can afford to go to college and get the training they need to show what they can do. I happen to think that's worth spending time on. Just because I chose to become a baker does not mean that I tossed my business management degree into the nearest bin on the way into the catering college.'

She gave a small shoulder-shrug. 'Relax, Rob. The charity has a full-time administrator and a professional team running it. Any questions, talk to Sean. He has been through the details and offered the use of the Beresford for the event.'

Ah. So that was it. This girl thought that he was going to turn a charity auction into a Rob Beresford promotional event.

Was that really how she saw him? As a self-serving ego-maniac? Well, this day was just getting better and better.

And with that she extended her free hand towards him, her eyes locked on his. Her gaze was intense. Focused. 'We made a trade last evening. One personal appearance in exchange for bed and breakfast. I need to know that we still have a deal this morning and you are not going to walk out on us.'

Rob stared at the food, then looked up into those sparkling green eyes, and took her hand.

It was warm, small, and sticky and calloused, with long, strong fingers that clamped around his. This was no limp, girly handshake. This was the hand of a woman who cooked her own food, kneaded her own bread, and washed her own dishes. The sinews and muscles in her wrists and forearms were strong and toned.

He was accustomed to shaking hands with men and women from all sides of the building trade every day of the week in his job, but this was different. A frisson of energy, a connection, sparked through that simple contact of skin on skin.

'I gave you my word. I'll be there.'

Her fingers gripped his for a second longer than necessary before releasing him, her eyes darting to his. The crease in her forehead told him that he was not the only one to have felt it. But to her credit Lottie nodded towards his plate. 'Good. Now that's cleared up, why don't you enjoy your tart? You still look as though you need it. Tough morning?'

He paused before replying. 'Yes, actually, it has been a tiring morning, and I'm sure it's delicious but I don't eat cake.'

Lottie sniffed and tilted her head. 'Well, that's a shame. Luckily I am confident that with your extensive culinary expertise you will have observed that this is not cake. This is a tart, which I made today, in this kitchen. At some silly time of the morning.'

Lottie gave her ovens a finger wave, and then moved to sit down on the corner of the table, her arms folded. 'Speciality of the house. And nobody leaves this kitchen without trying my baking. Including you, Rob Beresford.'

Her eyes ratcheted down to the pastry, then slowly, slowly, came back up to his face. 'I have heard the words and shaken on it, but now I want to see the proof that you want to cooperate with me. The success of the evening all depends on what you do in the next five minutes. So, what's it going to be, Rob?'

What Lottie had not expected was for Rob to reach out towards her. She forced herself not to back away as Rob picked up her left hand and kissed the backs of her knuckles before releasing it with a grin.

'We came to an arrangement. And a Beresford man always keeps his promises.'

Lottie uncrossed her arms and wrapped her fingers around the coffee cup as Rob glared at her for a second before picking up his fork and breaking off a piece of warm, fragrant tart.

Lottie Rosemount had no intention of letting the scholarship students down when it came to the simple matter of organising a fundraising event.

The last thing she needed was a celebrity chef turning up and questioning her abilities.

Even if that chef smelt of warm spice and looked as if he had stepped down from a photo shoot for a fashion magazine. She had never met anyone who could totally rock designer denim jeans and a white shirt.

Her eyes could not move from his wide, full lips wrapping around the cake fork.

She had to see his reaction when he tasted the combination of sweet almonds and warm spice with the aromatic juicy fruit of the ripe pear, which she had poached gently in spiced pear juice syrup until it was almost falling apart.

It had taken six trial batches before she was happy with the variety of pear and the cooking time.

Ah. There it was.

Rob's eyes fluttered closed for just a fraction of a second and then he chewed a little faster so that he could break off a huge piece of tart with his fork and pick it up with his fingers.

Oh, yes. He had got it. He liked it!

He was staring into her eyes now, the corners of his mouth turned up with a flicker of something that could have been amusement, interest, or more likely frustration that she had forced him into agreeing to come to the fundraiser.

A slight twinge of guilt flickered through her mind. She had been quite shameless. One overnight stay for a distressed artist in exchange for an hour shaking hands and supporting the charity. That was not too terrible. Was it?

'Mmm,' he murmured and drained the last of his coffee. 'Not bad. In fact, seriously good. Where did you say you trained?'

'Here and there. I finished my apprenticeship with Valencia Cagoni when you fired me. You can check the rest on my website later.'

The creases in the corners of his eyes deepened as Lottie inhaled a powerful aroma of spicy masculine sweat, which was sweet even against the perfume of the fruit and nuts in her food.

His gaze hovered over her ring finger, then flicked back to her face, eyebrows high.

'Not married? Or are you too rebellious to wear a ring?'

Lottie almost choked on a piece of pastry from her tart and quickly swallowed down a slurp of coffee before wheezing out a reply.

'Not married, engaged, dating, or anything else. Where would I find the time for that?'

'If you wanted it enough you would find the time.' His eyes flashed a challenge that was definitely hot enough to warm the coolest of breezes.

Wanted it? Oh, she wanted it. But it had to be the right man who wanted the same things. And so far they were thin on the ground.

'Not very high on my priority list at the moment,' she lied, but not very convincingly because that smile on Rob's face lifted into a knowing smirk of deep self-satisfaction.

Damn. She had fallen straight into his trap.

'So it's all work and no play for the lovely Miss Rosemount. That doesn't sound like much fun.'

'And your life is one great circus of constant amusement because your business runs itself. Is that right?'

Damn him for making her snappy.

'I never said that,' he replied with a twist of his head towards the door where a young couple was staggering in with a baby buggy and shopping bags.

She couldn't move. There was something electric in the few inches of air between them, as though powerful magnets were pulling them together.

At this distance, she could feel that frisson of energy and strength of the man whose whole professional life had been spent under the glare of public scrutiny—by choice.

This was the kind of bloke who was accustomed to walking into a cocktail bar or restaurant and having head waiters fawn over themselves to find him the best table.

Well, not this time, handsome!

She could stick this out longer than he could.

It was Gloria who saved him. Her friend came galloping down the stairs from the bedroom and third-floor studio and instantly twisted her mouth into a smile.

'Well, hello! You have to be Rob. You mum has been telling me *all* about you, scamp. I'm Gloria.'

With a laugh she turned to Lottie. 'Adele decided to take her breakfast to the studio with Ian. They're having a great time up there so I thought I would leave them to it.'

There was a sharp intake of breath from across the table. 'Ian?'

'My friend Ian Walker,' Lottie said. 'You must have met him last night. He was the photographer who worked with your mum on the exhibition catalogue for the gallery. Tall, thin, about forty. And a great fan of your mum's work.'

Suddenly Rob was standing ramrod-straight next to her, his back braced, and looking horribly tall, as though he feared the worst.

'Then I think it's time I caught up with them, don't you?' he said. 'So you have a studio?' he went on. 'That is different. I have been to plenty of artists' studios in my time but above a bakery? My mum and her pals would spend more time scoffing the goods than working.'

Her mouth opened and then closed before she answered him with a smirk. 'Ah. So this is going to be a first. And who said anything about artists? Prepare to be disappointed. Follow me.' Then she caught his smile and her eyes narrowed. 'On second thoughts, you can go first. Straight through that door. Then at the top of the stairs take a sharp left and carry on up to the third floor. You can't miss it.'

Rob took the stairs two at a time then slowed down to take the narrow second steps, conscious that Lottie was by his side the whole time.

His mother was alone with a man who he had never met; he certainly did not recognise the name. In his book, that meant trouble. *Lots of trouble.*

Especially when they stopped outside what looked like a bedroom door.

Lottie stepped forwards and gently turned the brass handle, casually swung open the wooden door and stepped through.

The walls and ceiling were painted in brilliant white.

Light flooded in from the plain glass windows, illuminating one single picture hanging over what must have been the original chimney breast.

Staring back at him was a life-size formal portrait of Lottie Rosemount—the impact of seeing her captured knocked Rob physically backwards.

He was so stunned that it took a few seconds for him to notice that Lottie had moved forwards and was chatting to a tall, thin, older man, who he vaguely recognised, standing next to a long table covered with a pristine white cloth.

His quick brain struggled to take in what he was looking at.

It was the complete opposite of what he had been expecting.

Instead of the chaotic blend of noise and bakery odours and general chaos he had walked into in the cake shop, the third-floor space was a haven of quiet sunlight and calm.

It was a separate world. *An oasis.* And totally stunning.

The studio had clearly been a loft and the ceiling was angled away into one corner, but half of the roof was made from glass panels, which created a flood of light into the centre of the room. The outside wall had two wide panels of floor-to-ceiling double patio doors. And sitting outside on a tiny patio chair, cradling a large white cup, was his mother.

She was wearing a silk kimono, her hair was already styled, and there was a china plate stacked high with *pain au chocolat* and Danish pastries, which he knew that she adored. Next to an open box of tissues.

'Darling. There you are! What a lovely morning. Do come and look at this wonderful view. Isn't it divine?'

Rob rolled back his shoulders and, with a nod to Lottie and Ian, who were totally engrossed in looking at some images on a laptop computer, walked out onto the narrow roof terrace.

He pressed his lips to his mother's hair and wrapped his arm loosely across the back of the chair as she blew her nose.

'How are you this morning, Mum? Cold any better?'

'Much. I have it down to sniffles. And I slept for hours! Hopefully I shall stay awake at the gallery today when the great British public arrive. It was such a shame that I did not last much of the evening.'

He rested his chin on her shoulder so that they were both looking out at the same panoramic view across the London skyline towards the river Thames.

'Now, tell me what you have been up to this morning.'

Perhaps it would be better not to mention last night after all.

His breath caught in his throat.

All of the Beresford hotels in the city had views over London, but this? Somehow being on this tiny terrace reminded him so much of the house where he had grown up with his dad. The window box full of red geraniums. The wrought iron railings. The tiled clay roofs that spread out with the old chimney pots. Church spires. And the faint sound of the busy London street just below where they were standing. Red buses, black cabs. The whole package.

He had missed this. He missed the real London.

'Couldn't have put it better myself,' he whispered. 'This is special.'

'It's wonderful. How clever of you to persuade your friend to allow me to stay here. Because I have to tell you, darling, your hotel is charming and so efficient but this place is divine and Gloria and Lottie have been perfect hosts. And the studio…'

Adele pressed one hand gently to the front of the kimono and Rob was shocked to see the faint glimmer of tears in her eyes.

'When I first came to London your father tried so hard to find me somewhere to work and the closest I came was somewhere just like this. A third floor of an old stone house that had belonged to one of the Impressionists. I loved it, for a while.'

Then she waved one hand. 'It was not to be, but that is past history and there is no point living with regret. Strange, I had almost forgotten how special this city is.'

'London? I thought that you hated it here.'

'Hated it?' his mother replied and turned around to face him. 'Oh, no, darling. I could never do that. I was so young and I simply couldn't find my balance.'

Then she looked out across the rooftops. 'We've both come a long way since then, kiddo. A hell of a long way.'

A killer grin lightened her face. 'This is wonderful and I intend to enjoy every minute of it before heading back to the gallery. So scoot. Go and talk to Ian. That man worked miracles with my catalogue and Lottie needs your help. Call me before you go. But in the meantime, I am simply splendid.'

And with that she snuggled back in the chair and picked up a flaky pastry and bit into it with moans of delight.

It was the happiest that he had seen her for weeks.

Well. So much for all of his concerns about finding his mother a wreck!

Perhaps he had to thank Lottie Rosemount for a lot more than he'd first thought.

He loved his mother very much.

Lottie exhaled slowly as the thought crept into her mind that she had made a horrible mistake.

She darted a quick glance towards the terrace where Adele was quite happily enjoying the June sunshine with Rob chatting so sweetly by her side, his arm draped so protectively close, and swallowed down a moment of deep humiliation.

She had been wrong.

Last night had not been about Rob trying to save his credibility and reputation at all.

It had all been about protecting his mother. Not himself.

That was why he had been so concerned about going to the hotel.

He had been terrified that his mother would embarrass herself and the press would be full of photographs of Adele staggering about looking half drunk and falling out of a limo onto the street in front of the cameras.

How could she have been so stupid?

When Rob Beresford had walked into that art gallery all she had been able to see was the man who had treated her so unfairly.

But what about the rest? It was gossip. Tittle-tattle scandal about Rob's many conquests and how he had ditched Debra without a moment's notice.

A low icy shudder ran across her shoulders.

She was a fool. No, worse than that. She had allowed her memory of what had happened when they had last met to cloud her judgement.

This was not just unfair, it was wrong.

Stupid, stupid, stupid.

She had made a total fool of herself by doing the very thing she'd promised she would not do again: judge people based on what they had done in the past.

And if she was guilty of that she was woman enough to put it right.

Right now.

'Rob.' Lottie smiled and strolled over to the terrace. 'Can I drag you away from Adele for a moment? You're an expert on recipe books and this is my first. Do you remember Ian? This lovely man has bravely taken on a very different kind of challenge: making my novelty birthday cakes look good enough to eat. Welcome to my budget photo shoot!'

On a white cake stand on a pedestal in the middle of a long table covered in a white cloth was a cake.

It had been shaped into a racing car Rob vaguely recalled seeing on movie posters for a children's cartoon film some months ago.

The long low body was covered with bright red fondant icing with a white stripe running down both sides. The wheels were white discs and the whole design looked so realistic it might have been mistaken for a toy. Except that Lottie had just finished icing liquorice round sweets in place of the headlights and steering wheel.

All in all a perfect cake for a car-mad little boy.

It was brilliant.

Rob stepped closer and nodded to Ian, who stopped work

adjusting a light stand and an elaborate studio camera system on a tripod to come forward and shake his hand. 'Good to meet you, Rob. Adele has told me a lot about you.'

'Really?' Rob answered and glanced towards his mother, who was now chatting happily to Lottie and eating croissants. *Because she has not said a word about you.* 'Congratulations on the exhibition catalogue. Everyone I spoke to last evening loved the layout.'

'It was my pleasure.' Ian shook his head. 'Although I confess that I didn't expect to meet Adele here this morning when I turned up to work on the charity cookbook Lottie is pulling together. Do you have an interest in food photography, Rob?'

'Me? Not at all. I leave that to the experts. I simply prepare the food and the stylists and photographers get to work on the recipe books.'

He quickly scanned the room, taking in the high ceilings and natural light from the skylight and tall windows. 'Has this always been a photographer's studio?'

'Not as far as I know. Lottie refurbished the loft as soon as she bought the place. It is quite something. And I need to get back to it or the cake will dry out. Later.'

A quick tour of the loft revealed that Lottie's taste in books ranged from classic French cuisine to high finance and shared the space with a fine collection of spiders' webs and dust.

At the far end, away from the windows, was a screened-off area, and Rob could not resist peeking behind the découpage screen.

A double bed with a Victorian carved wooden headboard was flat against the wall. Dressed with white bedcovers trimmed in lilac satin and a soft-looking duvet.

Feather. He could tell from the way it was made.

Hmm, interesting. He wouldn't be trying that bed out. Way too girly.

But who slept in a bed that size?

He was just about to investigate when there was a sharp cough from behind his back. 'Found anything interesting back there,' Lottie asked and he knew without bothering to look that she had her hands on her hips, 'Mr Nosy Parker?'

'My natural, insatiable curiosity cannot be contained, Goldilocks.'

'Goldilocks? What do you mean?'

Rob peeked at her over one shoulder and smiled. 'Thought so. I have discovered your secret hideaway. Not a bad spot. Not bad at all.'

'Actually, it's lovely. I don't mind sleeping in the studio for six months during the summer. It's not such a bad place to wake up in the morning.'

'And the rest of the time?'

Lottie strolled over to the screen and gestured to the terrace where Adele was just finishing off her breakfast.

'When I was in business my first Christmas bonus paid for an apartment in the city with a view over the Thames. At the moment I am renting it out to one of my former colleagues while she is working on a project in central London and wanted a home rather than a serviced apartment.'

Lottie dropped her hand. 'You know the statistics about how many restaurants and cafés never make it to their first birthday? Well, I am just coming up to eight months and—' she tapped on the wooden frame on the screen '—so far, so good. But who knows? Things change. People change.'

Then she paused. 'What gave me away?'

Then he gestured with his head towards the garment bags and clothing hanging on two garment rails behind the decorated screen. 'Designer clothing is not really Dee's style.'

'I could have put my clothes in storage but I prefer to have them handy. A girl has to be ready for all eventualities.'

'Is this what you are wearing on Saturday evening?' Rob picked up the skirt of a stunning slinky mocha-coloured satin slip with a lace trim and lifted his eyebrows before releasing it. 'Because I am not sure the Beresford Richmond is ready for this kind of allure. Va va boom.'

'Please don't touch the frillies. And my gown is going to be a surprise, so do stop looking.'

'Fair enough. What time shall I pick you up?'

'That's okay. I'm meeting you there.'

'Why, Miss Rosemount, surely you are not frightened of tongues wagging if we walk in together, are you?'

'Not at all. But I am going to get there early to help set things up. That's all.'

'Is that it? Or do you have a rule about not dating chefs?'

'Dating? Of course not. I don't have any problem with chefs. Far from it. I have spent three years working my backside off becoming one.' Her gaze locked on to his chest but slowly, slowly, lifted to his face. 'Just arrogant chefs with egos to match the size of their name on the menu.'

Lottie gave a small shoulder-shrug. 'Any girl who dates a chef who likes to have his name in the gossip columns knows what she is taking on and I am not just talking about the long hours and bad tempers.'

'Harsh. You could say that about any type of successful person, the kind that has earned that reputation through sweat and puts the work in for that success. Publicity is not a bad thing. Not when restaurants are closing every week. The press love me just as long as I give them something to write about. It's part of the job.'

'Ah. Well, there you have it. You can glory in the glare of publicity for the charity and we lesser mortals shall scurry around in the background making sure that everything is working. Win-win. I can hardly wait. It promises to be a very interesting evening.'

CHAPTER SIX

It was like going back in time.

Rob Beresford stood at the entrance to the park across the street from the West London Catering College where he had spent two of the most gruelling years of his life learning how to cook at a professional level.

The building might look a little cleaner and they had added more glass and pale colours to the entrance to make it look less like a prison, but otherwise it was just the same.

Somewhere in a storage unit in London there was a box stuffed with his diplomas and degree certificates for what the college liked to call the culinary arts and professional cooking.

From what he remembered it was mostly culinary sweat and manic activity fuelled by industrial quantities of cheap coffee and cheaper carbohydrates.

He had grown up in London and spent the first nineteen years of his life here. It would always feel like home.

And now he was going to a Beresford hotel to raise funds so that some other youngster with nothing but a fire in his belly could have a chance to show what they could do.

How ironic was that?

With a low chuckle he shook his head and strode out along the sunlit pavements and turned the corner, away from the college and into the world he lived in now. Sean had done a great job refurbishing the Beresford Richmond and Rob waved to the reception staff as he jogged up the staircase to the main conference room and flung open the doors to the cocktail bar.

He scanned the room looking for Sean or Lottie and walked slowly between the drinks tables, waving and saying a brief hello to familiar faces from the hotel and food world, flashguns lighting up his back as he tugged at the cuffs of his evening shirt.

He was a Beresford working the crowd in a Beresford hotel.

This was the one time he was willing to put his handmade tux on show for the press and wear his heart on his sleeve.

His father, Tom Beresford, had founded the Beresford hotel chain from nothing and worked hard to create a line of luxury hotels in cities around the world. But Rob admired him for a lot more than that. No matter where his mum had gone to find artistic inspiration, his dad had made sure that Rob had his own room and a stable home and school life. It had been a shock when his dad had announced that he was going to marry again. Until then it had only been the two of them. But she was so lovely. And as a bonus—he got a new brother.

And there he was. Sean Beresford. Hotel troubleshooter and the current manager of the hotel he was standing in, greeting the sixty or so especially invited guests in person, same as always. Charming but professional.

Rob took the initiative by thumping Sean on the back in a half hug. 'Heard that there was a charity auction tonight and thought I might pick up a few bargains. How about you?'

He was rewarded by a short snort. 'Dee is in China. Again. But somehow Dee and Lottie persuaded me to host

their fundraiser here. I even agreed to be the master of ceremonies. So behave.'

'I am behaving! And well done on the refurbishment.
This is a fabulous venue.'

'Thanks. Hard work but worth it. VIP events like this
are a perfect way to get word-of-mouth publicity. Gold
dust. I had no idea that Lottie knew so many people in
high places.'

His brows came together. 'Lottie Rosemount?'

'Absolutely. That girl has a contact list to die for. If anyone deserves praise for making this benefit a sell-out it's
Lottie. Oh, have to go. Enjoy the party! And I hope you
like the food. We're trying that new event menu from the
Beresford Paris which has been so popular.'

'Wait up. What are you serving? Surprise me.'

'Canapés followed by plated cold starters, three choices
of hot buffet, salad and cheese. And I know you are going
to sample some of everything because you always do before the desserts arrive.'

Sean gestured with his head towards the swing doors
that led to the kitchen. Waiters were clearing away what
little was left of the patisserie.

'I have a head chef in there who has been screaming at
her brigade all night that Rob Beresford is in the room and
they had better cook as though their jobs depended on it.
Forget the other city chefs. You are the one my team want to
impress. They are nervous wrecks in there! So don't worry
about the food. Your job is to do the celeb thing. And good
luck with that. See you later.' And with that Sean strode
over to greet the cluster of new arrivals who had packed
the reception area behind him.

Rob stepped to one side, and tried to bring his breathing
back down to a level where he could control it.

What the hell was the new event menu from Paris?

He was supposed to be responsible for the entire food-and-drinks range across all of the Beresford hotel chain.

His mother's exhibition and the filming of the TV show had sucked every second of his life for the past few months but surely he would have heard about a new menu?

Why had no one told him about it? Or worse. They had told him but the message had got lost in the hundreds of emails he received every day.

Of course he had to trust the hotel chefs. He had personally picked them, got drunk with them and slayed them with cooking better than them. But as for trusting other people to create an entirely new menu? Forget it.

He needed to get to the hotel kitchens and find out exactly what they intended to serve at this function.

He glanced around the gilt high-ceiling dining room. Top hoteliers, company directors in designer suits, food journalists and, if he was not mistaken, several of the college lecturers who were responsible for what skills he had. So overall pretty much everyone in London with an interest in developing amazing new chef talent.

Brilliant for the charity. And a nightmare waiting to happen if this new menu was not totally spectacular.

And walking towards him around the edge of the room, one very, very pretty girl.

Lottie Rosemount. Only not the hard-working baker version of Lottie he had spent most of the day with.

This Lottie was dressed in a pale lilac cocktail dress that fitted her perfectly, the fabric draped close to her waist then flaring out over the slim hips to just above the knees. Then long, slim but muscular legs and high heels.

Tonight Lottie Rosemount was every bit the young female corporate mover and shaker he had seen at parties all over the world. Efficient. Brilliant. Organised.

Only he knew the real Lottie. The woman who had

taken a high-street bakery and transformed it into something spectacular. Doing what she loved to do, her passion. On her own terms.

When had he last met a woman like that? Not often. Oh, he had met plenty of glossy-haired girls with high IQs who had claimed they were doing what they truly loved, and plenty of lady bakers had studied business, but so few people were able to combine the two skills to create a successful bakery.

Lottie had.

Maybe that was why he connected with the elegant, stunning woman he was looking at now, though he had only met her a few days earlier.

They were different from other people.

Her life forces, her energy, sparkled like the jewels in the bracelet on her wrist. She was effervescent, hot, and so attractive he had to fight down that fizz of testosterone that clenched the muscles under his dress shirt and set his heart racing.

Just at the sight of her.

Rob watched Lottie chatting away to the other guests. He heard her speaking and replying to questions in French and what sounded like Russian. Of course. She must have studied modern languages for business.

He headed for the bar, anxious not to make a fool of himself, ogling the woman in the lilac dress, but she strolled across through to the other room, totally confident and completely at ease in this group of top decision makers in the catering world. It was the kind of ease that came from an expensive education. Hadn't she mentioned something about a management degree?

It was an education designed to open doors. And it had.

His education had been at the school of hard graft and a local college that would take in a boy with a police record and next to no academic qualifications past the age of seventeen.

He picked up a glass of sparkling water and turned back to the cluster of other guests at the same moment as Lottie started introducing some tough-looking lads to one of the college lecturers he vaguely recalled from his student days, going out of her way to make them feel relaxed and included.

He had got it wrong.

She was not one of the hobby bakers who opened a cupcake shop for a joke. A whim to keep her and her friends amused and give them somewhere to meet up to laugh at the poor schmucks who had to slave for a living.

Just the opposite

She had trained. Worked. Slaved. Knew what she was talking about.

People did not often surprise him, not after years in the hotel trade.

Lottie Rosemount was one of a kind.

Perhaps that was why his gaze stayed locked solid on that lovely face until she turned and strolled away towards the stage on Sean's arm to begin the charity auction, leaving Rob to stare after her. And the low back of her dress.

Whoa. Mind-blowing. Brain-blasting whoa.

What had he intended to do? Oh, yes. Find out what the hell was going on with this new menu he knew nothing about.

He caught sight of a waiter emerging from the kitchen with a platter of canapés. Then another, and another. His heart instantly sank. It was too late.

The food service had started. There was no way he was going to barge into that kitchen and start asking questions when the food was already on plates.

Plan B. He was going to have to find out the hard way.

By tasting every single dish presented to the guests at this event. And they had better be spectacular. Or he would want to know why.

'Well. What did you think?'

'I think he did a fine job.' Lottie smiled, her gaze focused on the stage. 'Consider me impressed. But don't you dare tell him that I said that. The students are thinking of joining his online fan club and they must have taken at least a hundred photos on their mobile phones.'

Lottie stood shoulder to shoulder next to Sean and they watched in contented silence as Rob chatted and laughed with the newest group of catering students. He had spent most of the last hour following the charity auction happily introducing the wide-eyed students to chefs who Lottie had held in awe for most of her life. Chefs who she had somehow managed to get to donate seven-course dinners as auction prizes were like putty in Rob's hands.

'There is one tiny little thing which I should mention. Did Rob come up with tonight's menu?'

Sean shook his head. 'Rob is responsible for the hotel standards but the executive chef at the Paris hotel sent over the recipes.'

Lottie slowly produced a printed copy of the menu that she had stolen from the table and passed it to Sean who groaned out loud.

'Oh, great, what's this? Marks out of ten? And what are these scribbles down the side and over the page?'

'Suggestions. Ideas. Proposals. And when it comes to that mess of a salad, a shut-down notice. Pomegranate seeds on the same plate as chopped walnuts, anchovies and smoked ham? It was a mess. But the rest?'

Lottie flipped the flat of her right hand from side to side

and sucked in air between her teeth. 'It was edible. But that is all I could say about it.'

Sean coughed. 'Don't hit me, but it sounds like you might enjoy working with that brother of mine and coming up with your own recipes.'

'Work with the mighty Rob Beresford? The very idea. I'm far too good. His ego would never recover.' Then she laughed and nudged Sean in the arm. 'Let's go talk to your chef and hear what she has to say about tonight's meal. I'd like to hear what she thinks.'

Then Lottie paused and shot a quick glance back towards the stage and her voice faded away. 'But after that I need to catch up with Rob about a very interesting phone call that I have just had with Valencia Cagoni. Your brother has some explaining to do.'

Sean snorted out a reply. 'Too late. He's seen you and is coming this way. Best of luck!'

Lottie lifted her chin as Rob sauntered over with a couple of students and waved towards the buffet table where a few remaining desserts were being demolished by the students before they were cleared away.

A wave of conflicting emotions coursed through her at the sight of his handsome face smiling at her. Confusion, disbelief, annoyance, and something alarmingly like respect were in the mix.

'Hi,' she said in a very hoarse voice, then covered it up with a quick cough. 'Fed up with signing autographs yet?'

'They're a great bunch.' Rob nodded and half turned to face the buffet. 'You were right about the scholarships. Half of those young men wouldn't be here if their fees were not paid. Good idea. I like it.'

He rolled his shoulders back and shoved both hands into his trouser pockets. 'I like it so much I am going to do something about it. Leave it with me. I'll come up with something to give that fund a boost.'

'Really?' Lottie squeaked. 'That's fantastic. Splendid. Great.'

There must have been something in her voice that made Rob turn and look at her.

'Are you feeling okay?'

'Never better. In fact I have just had the most fascinating chat with my old boss, Valencia Cagoni. Her twins are recovering from the chickenpox and she was delighted that I had found such an inspiring replacement chef for the fundraiser. But, of course, you know Valencia very well, don't you, Rob?'

Lottie whirled around and stepped closer to Rob so that the few remaining guests would not be able to hear their conversation.

'In fact, you know her so well that you sometimes pass on your personal recommendations for new apprentices in her restaurant.'

She took a breath and took one more step so that she could almost reach out and touch him if she wanted to. 'Apprentices like me.'

Her eyes narrowed. 'You were the one who persuaded Valencia to give me that training place. You made the call, you told her that I would be coming to see her and that she should give me a chance.'

'She told you.' Rob winced. 'Damn.'

Lottie stabbed Rob in the chest with her forefinger. 'You are responsible for my entire career. You!' Then she stepped back and looked around the ballroom. 'I still cannot believe it.'

His eyebrows lifted. 'Valencia Cagoni is an old friend from college. You needed a job in a hurry. I made the call. Happy now?'

'No, I'm confused.' Lottie blinked. 'Why didn't you just tell me that earlier and save yourself some grief? And Valencia never said a word. Not once in three years. She made me slave for that training post.'

'I asked her not to tell you that I had called,' Rob replied, and then dropped his shoulders back. 'You know how chefs talk. It makes it feel a lot sweeter if you had to fight for what you want and get it on your own merit, instead of who you know in the business. You had to work, and work hard. What you achieved was down to you, not me.'

Then he flicked one hand in the air. 'You know Valencia would never have taken you on unless she was convinced that you had talent. She is way tougher with her training than I am.'

'You fired me, and then set up my replacement training position. Why? Why did you do that?' Lottie asked, her voice trembling with emotion. 'I would really like to know because right now my head is spinning.'

'Because I knew Debra was never going to be a mentor to anyone with talent. You deserved a chance to show what you could do and Debra was not going to let another chef steal her star. Valencia needed someone who could step up. Okay?'

Lottie stared at Rob in stunned silence, her hands planted one on each hip, her gaze locked on to his eyes.

'Has anyone ever told you,' she breathed in a low voice 'that you are the most infuriating man alive?'

'Frequently.' He grinned. 'Has anyone ever told you that you are the prettiest and most persistent woman alive? Perhaps that is why I find you so intriguing.'

He glanced from side to side and then pushed out his elbow. 'We're done here. Might as well hit the road in style! How about it?'

Lottie glared at Rob's elbow, then at his face and then

back to his elbow, before sighing out loud and hooking her
arm through his.

'This has already been one crazy evening. Why not go
the whole way? Because I really don't know what to think
about you any longer. First I think you are a complete…
and then the whole image gets flipped over. It is so beyond
annoying it's not funny and it's giving me a headache just
thinking about it. I really don't have a single clue who you
are, Rob Beresford.'

'Want to find out?'

CHAPTER SEVEN

'IS THIS LEGAL?'

'Behave. I need to clear my head and the main entrance is too far away. Fancy a walk?'

Lottie stared at the wooden sign that read in large letters: 'Keep Off the Grass', inhaled sharply, pulled her arm tight towards Rob and stepped over the low wooden white fence that separated the London pavement from the grass in the public park.

It only took a minute to skip across the grass and onto the path but her heart was beating a little harder when they were back on tarmac.

'You don't like breaking the rules. Do you?' Rob smirked.

He was observant, too. 'Not something I do very often. But I suppose it is a lovely evening and my headache needs an airing. Why don't we take a tour of the park? I haven't been in there for years.'

And it *was* a lovely evening, and Rob Beresford looked hotter than fresh bread just out of the oven. He smelt just as good, too.

Her treacherous heart had not completely got used to the fact that she was strolling along the pavement arm in arm with this dazzling man as he casually chatted to her as though they were old friends out for the evening.

Occasionally Lottie had to fire a hot glance in Rob's

direction to make sure that she was not in fact hallucinating and this was the same man who breathed dragon fire at trainees and made grown men cry on TV.

The arrogance and attitude were gone and in their place was this astonishing man who she now knew was responsible for kicking off her career with the finest award-winning patisserie chef in London.

And the transformation knocked the feet out from under her.

'Ian was telling me about your idea for a birthday cake book. I like it. Could be fun.'

'I think so. My cake shop is right in the middle of the high street and these days a lot of mums and dads simply don't have the time or, to be honest, the skill, to come up with that perfect birthday cake. So I get a lot of orders. And you would be surprised at how many are for old-style family cakes for grandparents and even great-grandparents.'

'Are you kidding me?' Rob asked with a lilt in his voice.

'Nope. That's one of the reasons why I started the Bake and Banter club. To teach adults how to bake a cake they can make at home which the family will love.'

She shifted closer to Rob to avoid a group of tourists who had their heads down, totally engrossed in their tablet computers and oblivious to other people on the walkway.

'You really get a buzz out of the baking, don't you?'

'More than I ever expected,' Lottie replied with a smile. 'So far I have made eight versions of that cartoon–racing car cake you saw this morning for little boys aged four to eighty-four and they all love it. Everyone is so different. Take next week, for example. The baking club want me to demonstrate how to make a chocolate birthday cake for one of our regular customers. Ninety years young. She wants loads of soft gooey chocolate icing. And three layers of chocolate sponge in the middle. Eat with a spoon. Whipped cream on the side. Delish.'

'Oh, yes, I remember what it was like to have my hands in sticky icing sugar and chocolate all day. Don't miss it a bit. But let me tell you—' he tilted his head closer to hers and half whispered '—for a working baker, you look fabulous.'

'Thank you, kind sir. My pleasure. You clean up nicely yourself.'

Rob exaggeratedly tugged with one hand at the lapel of the same dinner jacket he had worn for the gallery opening, while dodging the other pedestrians on the busy west London pavements. 'Oh, this old suit? Thought I had better make an effort as the star pupil.'

Lottie gave his arm an extra squeeze before snorting out loud. 'Shameless! Make that one of the many star pupils! How is your mum's cold?'

'She's feeling a lot better today and went to the gallery this afternoon before heading off to tea with her pals,' Rob replied as he negotiated around some dog walkers. 'So I am officially off duty for a couple of hours and, unless you are desperate to get home, I think this calls for a small delay! Look across the street. What do you see?'

He slipped his dinner jacket around her shoulders and held her within it for a few seconds, bringing up the collar so that he could flip the ultra-soft fabric around her smooth neck.

She pretended not to notice as his fingertips gently moved against her skin to flick the ends of her hair back over the collar.

'Thank you.' She smiled back in reply, conscious that the hard cheekbones of Rob's face were highlighted too sharply by the streetlight outside the swish, glossy shopfronts. He was too lean, but she knew that he had eaten something from every tray of the buffet at the hotel.

Maybe she could do something about that, if he stayed around long enough.

He smiled and surprised her by sliding around behind her, so that his arms were wrapped around her waist, holding her tight against him. She felt the pressure of his head against the side of her face as he dropped his chin onto her shoulder, lifted his left arm, and pointed.

Lottie tore her eyes away from Rob, and stared across to a very familiar sunlit stone building. Then laughed out loud.

'It's the old grand entrance to the catering college. We've come around in a circle.'

Rob nodded and looked up into the high carved stone entrance to what had been a 1930s art deco school of architecture before it was taken over by the catering school.

'The first time I walked through those doors I was seventeen, angry, bitter, and furious with the world and myself. I was a mess, Lottie. And maybe not someone you wanted to be around.'

There was something is his voice that compelled Lottie to look over her shoulder into his face. This was the young man, so full of hope and dreams.

'Why do you think that you were such a disaster?' Lottie replied with a smile, looking into his face. 'From my experience, most seventeen-year-olds feel that way.'

'Oh, girl, if you only knew the truth of it.'

Then something shifted in his eyes as though a darker memory had floated up to the surface.

And in that moment the mood changed. His brow was furrowed with anxiety, his mouth moved back to a straight line, and his body almost bristled with tension.

'Then tell me. Tell me the truth about why you were such a mess, because I really want to know.'

'That's one hell of a long story.'

'Then let's sit down and look at the college and reminisce together.' She looked around and spotted an old and not very clean wooden bench, which she covered with Rob's expensive jacket, liner side up.

'Ah. This is perfect.' Lottie shuffled back on the hard seat and folded her hands neatly on her lap.

'It is June. It's a relatively warm evening and I am sitting on your jacket, so there is no possible escape. I suggest that you start at the beginning and go from there. That usually works.'

'Are you sure that you're not an art critic? Because you are being damn nosy.'

'One of my terrible character flaws; nothing I can do about it. Once I take an interest in something I have to find out everything there is to know. So fire away. Because I am not going anywhere until I find out why you were so very angry with the world the first day you walked through those doors.'

'A-ha. So you are interested in me. At last she admits it.'

'I want to know what kind of family my best friend is getting herself into. So far Sean has been great, but are there skeletons in the Beresford family cupboard which will burst Dee's bubble? Not going to happen.'

'Skeletons? Lottie, there is a whole pirate ship of skeletons moored offshore all armed to the teeth and ready and able to cause mayhem at any minute they are released. The problem is most of them are about my side of the family. Not Sean's.'

'I don't understand. Sean told me that your mum and dad get on just fine even though they're divorced.'

'They do. I am lucky. Tom Beresford met my mother when he opened up the first Beresford hotel in New York City. She was living a bohemian life in an artists' colony in the Hamptons most of the year, and holding exhibitions of her work in the city when she needed funds. Well...' Rob smiled. 'You've seen my mother. Gorgeous, fun, and so talented it's criminal. I don't blame my dad for falling for her one little bit. She was even more stunning back then and she must have really adored him to settle in the city. In the end they had six great years in New York before we had to move back to London to open the flagship hotel here. That was when things started to change. It was my mum who decided that she could not tolerate living here.'

'Did she hate London that much?'

'Not particularly. It was the sudden change in her routine that she hated. Mum likes her day and her life all laid out, nice and simple and familiar. London was too much, too fast, and she couldn't get used to it. In the end the only way she could work was to go back to the Hamptons for a couple of months at a time with frequent trips back to London to see me. I was only a toddler so I stayed here with my dad and got used to airports.'

'That must have been tough. But there are people who lead their whole lives like that. My dad used to boast that one year he spent a grand total of fifteen days sleeping in his own bed. The price of modern life.'

'It might have worked for your family but it didn't work for mine. My dad made plans to move back to New York but then my grandparents in Suffolk needed him and Mum was staying away for longer and longer periods...and they simply drifted apart. I was way too young to understand what divorce was and nothing really changed in my life. Until my dad met Sean's mum. Maria. And for the next ten years I found out what it was like to have a mother who was there every minute of the day when I needed her and who even gave me a brother.'

'Sean. Of course. You loved Maria. Didn't you?'

'Adored her. Oh, I knew that I had a real mother. At birthdays and Christmas the house used to be full of Adele Forrester and her friends and extended family who used to descend like a whirlwind then disappear again for another six months leaving chaos behind them. But that was the way Maria and my dad liked it. Open house. Maria was a very special person and Sean was great. I had a family who were willing to put up with a very confused teenager and help him make some sense of his life and what he wanted to do with it. It was all good. It was too good.'

Rob flicked his arm out in a wide arc towards the trees.

'And then it was all taken away from me. And I went off the rails. Big time.'

'Maria. Of course. I am so sorry. Sean told Dee that she had died when he was young.'

'Unfair. So very, very unfair. One day when Sean is a lot older you might want to ask him about his mother's life as a refugee fleeing war and destruction. Only to die of cancer in a country where she thought she was safe with a family she loved and loved her right back in return. Because I can't talk about it without wanting to hit something very hard.'

Rob reached out and nipped off a large leaf from the bush growing behind their heads and slowly tore it into segments with his long, clever fingers as he spoke.

'You want to know about my skeletons? I was seventeen years old, I had plenty of money and a driving licence, and enough fury and anger in my belly to burn down most of London. And that is precisely what I tried to do. I had grown up in this city and knew precisely where to find trouble and distraction in any shape or form. Drink, girls, gambling, and the kind of people my dad would throw out of his hotel. The whole package. Sometimes I got away with it by being smarter and faster than the other guy. Sometimes I didn't and I have a police record to prove it. And a few broken bones along the way. My nose was a different shape then.'

'What did your dad do? He must have been frantic and scared for you.'

'The best he could. He was grieving and lost. Sean was desolate. And I was out of control and heading downhill faster than he could apply the brakes.'

'How did you pull back from that life to find your way to catering college?'

'The hard way. I woke up one morning in the bed of a girl whose name I couldn't even recall and I must have had twenty messages on my mobile phone. All asking me to get back to the house. My mum had got herself into a mess in Thailand. And I mean a mess. Three hours later I was on a plane to Bangkok.'

Rob exhaled long and slow. 'I had heard the words *nervous breakdown* but nothing could have prepared me for the emotional wreck I found in a Bangkok psychiatric unit. Her latest lover had stolen everything she had and left her broke and alone in the middle of nowhere. It wasn't the first time that had happened but this was the worst. But she was lucky. One of the other artists on the retreat was worried about her and sent out a search party. They found her on the beach the next day. Crying. Distraught. Irrational and terrified of anyone touching her or coming near her. It was one of the worst twenty-four hours of my life.'

'Oh, Rob. That's horrific. For both of you.'

'I made her a deal. It was very simple. I promised that if she came back to London with me and got some medical help for her problems, then I would take care of her. I would go to college and get the qualifications I needed to run the hotel kitchens. Sober and clean, a hardworking little drone. And that is what I did. I poured all of that bitter anger and fury at Maria's death into my work.'

The shredded pieces of leaf fluttered through the air.

'That's why I am not surprised people found me scary. I was so desperate to prove that I could achieve something that I refused to allow anything or anyone get in my way. *Relentless* is actually not a bad description.'

'Did she agree? I mean, did she come back from Thailand with you?'

'My mum went into the best rehab unit money could buy and I already knew that she was going to be there a long time. My dad was going to see her when he could get away from the hotel business and Sean went along when the unit said that she was stable enough to cope. But apart from that it was just the two of us against the world. I thought that was going to be enough to get her through this dark time in her life and magically turn her back to the lovely mum I used to know and everything would be back to normal again.'

Rob shrugged. 'I was so naïve about mental illness. So wrong. Badly wrong. Things have never been the same. Oh, she can go for a year or eighteen months without a major episode, and then she will fall for some hotshot man and life will be wonderful—until it isn't. And I have to pick up the pieces and start all over again.'

Lottie hesitated before replying. 'The other night at the gallery. Was that what you were worried about? That it was all too much for her and she would have a relapse?'

'No. I was far more worried about what the killer combo of cold remedies and champagne would look like to the real critics who were standing outside with their cameras. A good news story about an artist who has come back after eight years with a wonderful inspirational show does not sell. But give them Rob Beresford's rehab-refugee mother? Oh, yes. Let's just say that I was tired of giving them what they want.'

Her fingers slid across the bench and found his. 'Then Adele is very lucky to have a son like you to protect her.'

'Is she? I haven't always been there for her, Lottie. Not by a long way. I had replaced her in my life with Sean's mother at the very time she needed me as a son. And that sort of guilt does not go away easily.'

'But you kept that promise. That means a lot in my book.'

Her own eyes pricked with tears, and she laced her fingers between his, forcing apart his fingers, which had tightened into a ball.

Her touch acted like a catalyst, and he ripped his eyes away from the park and focused on her face as his fingers relaxed and squeezed hers back, leaving it to Lottie to break the silence.

Lottie stopped and turned so that she was facing Rob. 'I have an idea. And you can tell me to mind my own business, but here goes.'

She took a breath. 'I can see that you want to help your mum become the best she can be. I want to help. She is a remarkable artist and I adore her work. If you like, she can use my studio any time she wants when you are in London together. Room service, accommodation and as much lemon drizzle cake as she can eat, courtesy of the management.'

She clenched her teeth and pretended to duck. 'What do you think?'

Rob looked into her face for a few seconds, before replying in a low intense voice.

'You would do that? For us?'

'In a heartbeat, yes.'

His reply was to take a firmer grip of her hand as he rose slowly to his feet.

'Thank you, Lottie. Yes. I think that she would like that very much. Although I should warn you, for a skinny artist that woman can eat a hell of a lot of cake.'

Lottie looked up into Rob's face and what she saw there was like a light in the darkness. He was not used to being shown kindness and was trying to bluff away the depth of his feeling.

Hell, she knew what that was like. She simply had not expected it in him.

And just like that the resentment she had held for the past three years and all of the imagined angst popped like a balloon. Gone. Finished. Over.

Time to start all over again with the Rob she was with right here and now.

Hesitantly at first, then more firmly, she grasped hold of both of Rob's hands and slowly let him help her up from the bench and back on her feet.

And with that they walked casually, hand in hand, in silence, along the wide path as though it were something they did all of the time.

Rob could never know that her palms weren't sweating due to the warm breeze, but the gentle way in which his fingertips stroked the tender skin. Her gaze moved over the happy groups of smiling, chatty couples who strolled across the park. Anywhere except Rob. She wanted to look at him so badly it was almost a physical pain.

Except that would mean giving in to the sigh of absolute pleasure that was bursting to escape.

This was what it would be like if she were Rob's girlfriend. On a regular date.

Except, of course, this wasn't a date, was it?

This was a kind gesture to his brother's friend, who had been in the right place at the right time to help him out with somewhere for his mother to stay. That was all it could be. All it was ever going to be.

So, why not enjoy these precious moments and make the best of them while she could? These were the happy memories *she* would hold precious over the coming months when Rob and Adele had gone back to their exciting, busy lives, and she was merely a person they might see at social events with Dee and Sean.

In a few days she would be back in her normal, safe life. Which was just how she wanted it, wasn't it?

Her brain was so distracted by the unfamiliar thoughts and feelings whirling around inside her head that she didn't see the sudden break in the paving slab until the toe of her thin-soled evening sandal caught in the stone and she found herself falling forwards, hands outstretched. Into a pair of strong arms.

It was seconds before her brain connected with the fact that she was standing chest to chest with Rob with both of his arms wrapped around her body, her hands flat against his shirt front.

Just for a moment, Lottie closed her eyes and revelled in the warmth and the strength of his embrace. The exquisite aroma of aftershave, antiperspirant and clean pressed linen. Lemon, blended with the musky spice of light perspiration of the warm summer evening, and something else, something unique. Rob. His scent, his heat. And the strange magnetic pull that made her want to edge closer and closer to him every time they met. The pull that was going to make parting from him so very painful.

The overall effect was so totally intoxicating, that suddenly she felt light-headed and bent forward to rest her brow on his chest.

This was her dream, her fantasy. For a few precious seconds she could pretend that she was just like any other girl out for a stroll with her boyfriend. Pretend that this man cared about her, had chosen her, wanted to be with her.

A strong bicep flexed next to the thin fabric of her dress,

and her eyes closed in pleasure. It had been so long since she had been held like this!

Drat Rob. Drat. She couldn't do this. Why had she agreed to walk with him? He would be flying back to his real world, and she would be back to square one. On her own, holding it together.

'Are you okay?' Rob asked, with enough concern in his voice to bring a lump to her throat again.

His hands slid down as she pulled back and smiled up into his face, but instead of stepping away he simply linked his hands behind her back, holding her in place as she recovered.

'Yes. I think so.' She glanced down at her shoe. 'How clumsy of me. Thanks for stopping me from falling flat on my face.'

Lottie leant back so that she could focus only to find him smiling down at her, his eyes scanning her face from side to side, as though looking for something before speaking.

His lips curved back into a wide, open-mouthed smile, so warm, so caring that she was blinded by it. The warm fingers of one hand slid up her back as he dropped his head forward and nuzzled his chin against her hair. 'I'm pleased that I was here at the right time.'

Some part of her brain registered that she should make a response, and she forced herself to lift her chin.

Bad mistake.

Because at that precise moment Rob shifted his position and as she whispered, 'Thank you,' she felt the heat of his breath on her cheek. Lottie dared to slowly slide the palms of her hands up onto his chest. She could feel the hard planes and ridges of his body beneath her fingers. Emanating enough heat to warm deep inside her, melting away the last remnants of icy resistance that might have lingered there.

A young couple walked by, then a cyclist, but Lottie could hear nothing except the sound of Rob's breathing as his lips pressed against her temple, and the stubble on his chin rasping against her cheek for a second before he released his grip on her waist and slowly, slowly, slid his hand up inside his jacket, and onto the bare skin of her back above her dress

The sensation was so unexpected, so delicious that she inhaled sharply, gasping in air.

It was as though she had given him a signal of approval.

As his fingertips stroked her skin his soft, sensuous mouth slid slowly and tenderly against her upper lip in the sweetest, most gentle of kisses. It was so brief that Lottie had only seconds to close her eyes and enjoy it before he pulled away from her, his fingers sliding down from the small of her back.

Leaving her feeling bereft.

'Would you like some coffee? I know the perfect place.'

CHAPTER EIGHT

'I COULD NEVER get tired of this view,' Lottie murmured as she looked out from the patio outside the luxurious apartment over the rooftops of London in the fading dusk.

'Remarkable.'

Lottie looked over her shoulder at Rob, who was leaning on the kitchen-area worktop. Staring at her as though she were the most fascinating thing in the room instead of the view from the patio. Taunting her with one glance. How did he do that? She had met international bankers who could take lessons on how to make people squirm from Rob Beresford.

She felt like rolling back her shoulders and squaring up to him but somehow she suspected he would enjoy seeing how uncomfortable his ogling was making her feel.

The look he was giving her at that second could be classified as a fire risk.

For the first time since she walked out of the hotel elevator a quiver of alarm crossed Lottie's mind, making her breath catch in her throat.

What was she doing here?

She had worked with predatory sharks in banking and through her family most of her life and was well used to their tactics of luring the little fish into a shallow pool where they could not possibly escape.

This time she was the one who had voluntarily decided to enter the shark's territory with nothing more than her brain and her wit as protection. To do…what, exactly? Had she completely lost her mind?

Blinking away the butterflies of doubt and something close to alarm, Lottie watched as Rob broke his stare and strode over to the open-plan living space and shrugged off his dinner jacket, casually draping it on the back of a sofa.

The muscles underneath the fine fabric of his dinner shirt strained taut against the tug and flexed enough to make the hairs on her arms perk up.

And just like that the attraction she had felt towards him in the park sizzled and caught flame, making her inhale sharply and turn back to the patio.

By turning into the gentle breeze Lottie could feel the cool air calming the heat of her skin, and, reaching back, she lifted her long hair from her neck and let it fall onto her shoulders.

'Have you always lived in London?' Rob asked as he joined her at the metal railing, so close that their elbows touched for a second before he braced himself.

The heady muskiness of his aftershave blended with the coffee aromas and something on his skin that was so uniquely Rob to create a fragrance that was so addictive it should be banned. Lottie's chest lifted and fell as she indulged in the pleasure before she managed to pull together a reply.

'I spent some time in management school in America but apart from that, yes, I suppose I have.' Her gaze scanned the lights laid out before her. 'I love this city. I always have.'

'Then that is something else we have in common.'

Lottie let go of the railing and half turned to face him.

The light from the living room created a mosaic of shadows on his face, which added to the hard planes she knew were there.

London?

'I thought that you couldn't wait to get out of this city and your business was based in California? Your mother was telling me all about her wonderful studio home on the beach and...'

Understanding flooded in to replace disbelief and Lottie turned back to face the panorama in silence.

Now she was getting a clearer picture of this man. Remarkable award-winning chef moves to California to be close to his mother when she needs him. And in the process starts a new career in TV. Still a player. Still someone interested in what was in it for him...but...

'She seems very happy there.'

'She is. The exhibition is a hit and my mum is heading back to California as soon as it closes and the next lucky artist takes over. Which means that it is back to work for both of us. I probably won't be back in London for a good few months.'

'Wow. Do you have a home of your own to go back to?'

'If you mean bricks and mortar and a welcome mat? Not exactly. I've claimed the penthouse in the Beresford Plaza and my mum has a loft packed with boxes of my old stuff. Is decaf okay for you?'

'Perfect. Thank you.'

Rob strolled back into the kitchen, topped up his elaborate coffee maker with water, and added two large scoops of ground coffee from a canister, before pressing several buttons.

'Well, I can see your barista skills are just fine, but do you still find time to cook, Rob? You must miss running your own kitchen.'

His hands stilled on the worktop. 'Cooking as in chopping veg and making stock? Not for years.' Then he grinned. 'I have the fun of bringing new chefs into the hotels and seeing them learn and grow and do amazing things. Every one of them is so desperate to impress me they give us their all. Now that *is* magical.'

Lottie strolled back into the apartment as he spoke and every word seemed to penetrate her heart and touch something very deep inside her. This was the closest she had come to the real Rob Beresford. No pretence. Just Rob standing in a kitchen waiting for coffee to brew after a night at a function where he played a clever version of the persona he had created for the outside world to see.

And yet here she was. Alone with him. And suddenly that very idea became so heady with the rush that she deliberately stepped back one step so that she could look at him from the side.

Desperate to keep just out of the effective range of his devastating power of attraction that was sucking her closer and closer by the minute.

'So you understood what I was trying to do tonight? Raise funds to make that dream possible?'

Rob swirled one hand into the air around his head. 'Of course I understood. Lottie, the fairy godmother, wants to make sure that she has the support in place before she makes commitments that could change someone's life. No false promises. That makes sense to me.'

'Fairy godmother? I bet you say that to all the girls.'

Lottie gave a mini curtsey. This was a mistake.

Because at that precise moment Rob raised his arms to lift a tray from the shelf, and in the process his shirt rose high enough above the waistband of his low-rise smart trousers to reveal a couple of inches of toned, flat stomach.

Why was it that she had always been attracted to the athletic type?

Just when she thought that he could not be more gorgeous, he had to hit her with this. The irony of it all made her sigh out loud.

Bad head.

Bad heart.

Bad need for contact with his man.

Bad, full stop.

'What? Was it something I said? Or have you found a new hobby down there?'

Lottie hesitated before replying, desperate to avoid the harsh truth, so she started gabbling instead of ogling.

'I love my bakery so much it's hard to imagine living in hotel rooms full time, no matter how splendid the view.'

Rob chuckled. 'Don't worry about it. I'm used to living out of a suitcase.'

For a moment she wanted to run into Rob's arms, feel the strength of his body against hers, and tell him how attracted she was to him.

But she wouldn't. Because he was leaving and she was staying, and that was a recipe for disaster in anyone's cookbook.

No. She had to control herself, and fight this powerful attraction. She just had to. His life was in the fast lane of the cities she had left behind her.

Time to put the mask back on, drink her coffee, and swallow down her feelings. And get the hell out of there before she did something stupid. Like pounce on him.

Lottie watched in silence as Rob poured the coffee.

'That smells divine.'

'Special import from one of the hotel's best coffee roasters. Oh, if you're hungry for dessert you'll find some soft amaretto biscuits in that tin. My Italian pastry chef claimed he made them himself, but I know your standards are pretty high so I await the expert opinion.'

Rob watched as Lottie flicked open the clasp on the steel canister and brought it up to her face, inhaling deeply.

'Oh, this is heaven. Did Dee tell you that I adore Italian food? Or did you have a premonition?'

'Serendipity. It seems that we share at least some of the same passions, Miss Rosemount,' Rob whispered as Lottie slowly closed her lips around a piece of the soft round almond-and-apricot biscuit and groaned in pleasure, her eyelids flickering as her face twisted in delight.

It was the sexiest thing Rob had ever seen in his life.

His chef was going to have to hire extra staff to cope with all of the takeaway orders coming to this apartment, because there was no way he was going to sit opposite this woman in a restaurant if she was going to act out a movie scene with her food.

He froze, stunned, as he tried in vain to control his breathing…and various other parts of his anatomy that seemed to have woken up to the fact that he was within arm's reach of an amazing woman, and they were alone in this apartment.

Once they recognised him as the chef who they had seen on the TV, women tended to either get stuck into the whole celebrity lifestyle and the second-hand fame that came with being photographed hanging on to his arm, or hit on him straight away for the extra points on the famous name scoresheet.

He gave them what they wanted and they gave him what he wanted. Simple, straightforward. No grey areas; always black and white.

Lottie was as multicoloured as a rainbow. She was totally unfazed by his star ratings and had challenged him from the first moment they met in the gallery.

He admired her for making him change his routine and cut out his usual public performance.

In fact, he liked that more than was good for him.

Maybe it was going back to the Beresford hotel and then the catering college, but the fact that she had crept under his guard tonight to the point where he had blurted out his life story rankled him deeply.

He never told his story. Not to the press and certainly not to strangers. It was way too risky and likely to end up in a tell-all story in some sleazy newspaper, which Sally would have to pay to suppress.

So what did that say about Lottie?

Could he trust her? Dee was a special girl and his brother adored her, but Lottie was very different. Clever, witty, and on the surface an excellent businesswoman.

After a lifetime in the hotel business he prided himself on being able to judge people and every instinct in his body was screaming at that moment that she was someone who had no guile or hidden agendas. And yet there was something sad lingering under that very lovely surface.

Hell. He knew all about that. But it was strange to see the sadness and regret so openly on Lottie's face when she thought he wasn't looking.

Even stranger, it made him all the more attracted to her.

His heart was racing, hard and fast, as he stepped across to the refrigerator to bring out the milk, and took a breath of cool air, fighting to regain his composure. This was getting out of hand, and all he was doing was looking at Lottie!

It had been a very long time since he had wanted to be with a woman as much as he did at that moment.

Lottie chewed and hummed gently to herself as he pretended to move the meagre contents of his huge refrigerator around.

Was this what it would be like to have someone who loved you, and wanted to be with you, not just for an afternoon between international flights, but seven days a week? He had only met this woman a few days ago, and the connection was... What was it? A crush? Because it was a lot more than physical attraction, that was for sure.

In a few days he would go back to his normal life across the Atlantic. This apartment would be rented out, and his time here would be a memory. Left to his imagination.

If this was what Lottie did with biscuits, what would she be like in his bed? Naked, with his hands running over the soft skin of her stunning body, giving her pleasure.

Suddenly Rob found an excellent reason to plunge his head inside the chiller.

'I have white wine if you would like some,' he asked, casually waving the sealed bottle the sommelier had sent up. 'Or perhaps a twenty-year-old tawny port?'

'Thank you, but I have to be up early tomorrow morning and I am already starting with a headache. This has been a long day.'

He closed the door and looked at her, slack jawed. 'You're serious. You are actually going back to work on a Sunday?'

'Of course. One of my very special customers at the bakery is celebrating her fiftieth wedding anniversary tomorrow and I promised that I would bake a very special decorated cake and deliver it in time for their tea party.' And without asking or waiting for a reply she dunked an amaretto biscuit in the hot coffee, slid off the stool, and held a piece of it in front of his mouth so quickly that without thinking he leant forward and closed his lips around her fingertips.

Sweet, warm, intensely flavoured almond exploded onto his taste buds. It was superb.

It was one of those special moments when the food and the company and the location came together and he knew that the next time he tasted that biscuit anywhere in the world he would remember how Lottie looked at that moment. Her face was flushed with excitement and sparkling energy, her lips warm and plump and soft, and those stunning eyes were focused completely on his face.

The silence between them opened up.

Then the coffee machine pinged to tell him the milk was hot and he swallowed, suddenly desperate to keep Lottie close to him as long as he could stretch out the precious time they had left together. 'I am going to have to give that man a raise. But tell me more about this cake of yours. Why is it so important to you?'

'Why? Oh, that's easy. Lily used to be our housekeeper and the woman who taught me how to bake. I owe my entire career to the one person who made my childhood bearable. I think that's worth a cake. Don't you? And these biscuits really are so good.'

She turned her back on him, scrabbling to open the spring lid on the canister, only her trembling fingers let her down and the biscuit fell to the floor.

Before Lottie could reach down to scoop it up, Rob stepped forwards and slid his fingers onto each side of her waist, holding her firm. Secure.

He breathed in an intoxicating combination of luxurious fragrance, body lotion, shampoo, and Lottie.

She smelt fabulous. Felt. Fabulous.

He dared to inch closer behind her, until he could feel the length of her body from shoulder to groin pressed against him.

His arms wrapped tighter around her waist, the fingers

pressing, oh, so gently into her ribcage, and he was rewarded by a gentle but tantalising low sigh.

Rob smoothed her hair away from her face so that he could press his lips against the back of her neck.

'Dee told me that you gave up your job in banking to spend your life doing something you loved instead,' he said, and his low soft voice seemed to resonate against the side of her head. 'That takes guts. And passion. If Lily gave you even a hint of that, then, yes, the lady does deserve the best cake you can make. Even on a Sunday. But why do I feel that you are only telling me part of the story?' He paused and slid just far enough way so that he could run his fingers back through her hair.

'Why did you really leave your old life behind, Lottie? What made you give up a well-paying job and take a risk on a bakery? You must have had choices.'

He sensed her shoulders lift with tension but waited patiently until she was ready to fill the silence. 'I did. If I'm honest, I had too many choices. My parents couldn't help. My dad wanted me to move to France and a ready-made slot in an IT company he had started as a retirement project. But not one person thought that I had it in me to retrain for a completely new career and start my own company. And that…hurt for a while.'

He swallowed down hard, stunned by the calmness of her voice, and pressed his chin against the top of her head. 'Then they didn't know you. Their loss.'

A deep chuckle bubbled up from inside Lottie's chest and he could feel it through his fingers. 'You're right. They didn't know the real me at all. My boss, my friends—even my boyfriend at the time—thought I would be back to work and my old life within six months. They were wrong. I love it. I sold enough shares to make it happen, but with Dee's help I think we created something very special. I *am* Lottie's cake shop now, and I wouldn't want it any other way.'

'So you gave it all up? Career, lifestyle, everything you had?'

'I traded up. Some of the happiest times of my teenage life were spent helping Lily in the kitchen, experimenting with pastry and flavours and textures.'

'Any regrets?'

'Some. I thought the friends I had made at school and university would stay my friends. But that didn't happen. Suddenly we didn't have anything to talk about any longer. Packing it all in and starting a bakery was what you did for a hobby when you retired, not your life's work. So I've had to make new friends instead.'

'Wait a minute. Your boyfriend didn't support you when you were going through so much upheaval?'

Rob slowly but firmly turned her around at the waist until his gaze was locked on that stunning face, his hands resting lightly on her hips.

'You are a beautiful woman, Lottie. He was a fool to let you go.'

Lottie smiled and pressed the flat of her hands on his chest before replying in a low, hoarse voice.

'He didn't let me go. We both knew that our relationship had come to an end. He wanted to climb the corporate ladder and achieve his dreams in banking. I didn't want that life any longer and he didn't understand how I could leave it all behind and start again on a shoestring. So don't judge him—that wouldn't be fair.'

'Then he was an even bigger idiot. Although it does make me wonder.'

'Wonder what?'

Lottie leant back within the circle of his arms so that she could gaze up into his face, and the compassion and need that Rob saw in those wide green eyes fractured the frosting of ice around his heart like an ice pick and kept on picking away until the warm and vulnerable core was exposed to the world.

It destroyed him. Broke him. Blasted away the shell that he had built up.

So that when he did reply, every word came from the heart instead of the head before he had a chance to change his mind.

'I was simply wondering whether you'd be willing to give another bloke a chance to show you how stunning you are. Is that so outrageous?'

Lottie inhaled a sharp breath and her gaze scanned his face as though she was looking for something. And found it.

'No. Not so outrageous at all.' She smiled.

'Excellent. Then why not start right now? Today. With me.'

Lottie's brain froze.

Him? Rob wanted her to start dating him?

He was holding out the most delicious temptation and all she had to do was say yes and find out if his touch was as exciting as she thought it would be.

For a night or even a weekend, if she was lucky, she would find out what it was like to be the object of a man's desire again.

Until he left. And she would be right back where she started. Alone.

Her gaze scanned his face. He was serious.

As serious as the most forbidden fruit could be.

'You don't know how to give up, do you?' Lottie said with a shaky smile.

'Not good enough for you?' Rob grinned back.

And then he nodded his head up and down, just once.

'Ah. I see your problem. You're too afraid you might get used to the idea of having a fling? Maybe even like it. Yup, could be trouble.'

'Come on, Rob. Your life and work is in California and you've already told me that you don't plan to come back to London any time soon. I have my bakery and right now there are no plans to open a cake shop and tea rooms in Carmel. So thank you for the compliment, but you know it would never work out. I'm not interested in long-term relationships.'

'Good. Because that's not what I am suggesting. In fact, just the opposite. My rules are pretty simple: a short-term relationship between two consenting adults, no strings and no expectation of anything more than what we have for as long as we have it.'

She looked into those eyes. Fatal mistake. It meant she was powerless to resist when he moved forward and pressed his long, slim fingers either side of her head and tilted his head to lean in.

His full mouth was moist and warm on her upper lip, and she could not help but close her eyes and luxuriate in the delicious sensation of his long, slow kiss.

Her arms moved around his neck, he moved closer, and she kissed him back, pressing hotter, deeper, the pace of her breathing matching his.

Somewhere at the back of her brain a sensible voice was shouting out that this was not a clever thing to do.

Bad Lottie. Very bad.

His lips slid away down her jaw to kiss her throat so she could gasp a breath.

'Take a chance on me, Lottie,' he whispered as his cheek worked his way down the side of her neck to her collarbone. 'I want to be with you, get to know you. Will you give me a chance to do that? Can you learn to trust me that much?'

She forced her eyes open wide enough to see that his own eyes were closed, his face…oh, his face. She was so going to regret this. One of her arms moved around so that she could run her fingers through his hair. 'I don't know. It would mean that you have to be around long enough to find out. Can you do that?'

He looked at her, his fingers pressing on her back.

'I will be around long enough. Will you give me a chance?'

She looked at him so long her stomach knotted up, his eyes scanning her face as though they were begging her to accept him. There was something in those eyes that went through her skin and penetrated her heart, blowing away any chance of resistance.

There was a lot to be said for giving in to impulses.

Lottie found herself grinning back at him, suddenly drunk with the smell, the feeling of his touch on her skin, the power of his physical presence.

Her fingertip traced the curved fullness of this man's lower lip, and his mouth opened a little wider at her touch.

Lottie stared up at Rob, into his sea-blue eyes, and knew that he wanted to kiss her again. She focused on his mouth as his long fingers stroked the sides of her face.

It terrified her. And thrilled her.

She wanted him to kiss her. To make the connection she longed for. There was no way that she could freeze this man from her life—it had gone too far now for that to happen. Her lips parted and she felt his mouth against hers as her eyes closed and she let herself be carried away in a breathless dream of a deep, deep kiss.

Tears welled up in Lottie's eyes and she tried to turn away as a single bead escaped but it was too late. Rob wiped it away with his thumb, the gentle pressure stroking her cheek with such tenderness it took her breath away.

How could she have doubted that this man was capable of being gentle and loving?

Yes, loving.

Her gaze scanned the cheekbones of his face, the bumpy nose, coming to rest on the bow of his upper lip above the full mouth. She felt as though she had known him all of her life.

Her fingertip moved over the crease lines in the corners of his mouth and eyes, which she knew now were down to more than just laughter.

Life had not been easy for this man. His love for his mother had driven him to take risks. If he had become ambitious it was not for his own ego. He had made sacrifices for the people he loved and would do so again.

His hand slid from her cheek into her hair. Smoothing it back from her face as his lips pressed against her brow, closer, and closer.

Her heart was racing, blood surging in her ears and she forgot how crazy this was as she closed her eyes and sensed the raw moistness of his lips on one eyelid, then the other. One of his hands moved around the curve of her waist, drawing her body closer to his.

The delicious sensation of being wanted as a woman dulled any sense of control she might have had left.

There was only this moment in time. There was only Rob.

She needed him as much as he needed her. How had that happened? And why did it feel so absolutely right to be in his arms, feeling his fingers stroke her back and hair, his lips on the crook of her neck, his chin pressed against her jaw? She knew she would be powerless to resist if the heat of that mouth moved closer.

She wanted him to kiss her again, and again, and her

head shifted so that she could caress his chin and cheek. Her lips parted and she felt the touch of his tongue on her neck.

Heaven was about to happen.

The pressure of his lips increased as he moved slowly under her chin and nuzzled her lower lip, back and forth, and she was lost in the heat of his embrace.

His hand slid down her arm and up to the hollow of her back, moving in slow circles on her skin at her waist, sending delicious waves of heat and desire surging through her body.

Her eyes closed with pleasure. He was so good.

There was a movement at her waist. He had started to work on the buttons at the back of her dress.

She wanted him to. She needed him to. She wanted… him to stop!

Something inside her screamed and she jerked her face away from his, her eyes catching a flash of his passion, his desire for her in that split fraction of a second before he realised that she was leaning back.

'I thought I was ready for this. Truly, I did.' She forced in a noisy breath. 'And I'm not. I am so sorry.'

His brows came together until understanding crept back into the rational part of Rob's brain and he exhaled, very slowly. A couple of times. Before refastening her buttons, single-handed.

His arm was still around her waist and he used his free hand to stroke her cheek as he drew her closer.

She cuddled into his chest, listening to the beat of his heart, knowing that she was the cause of the palpitations and smiling at the need. The smell of his sweat combined with his aftershave filled the air she was breathing.

Lottie pressed her lips together then closed her eyes and blurted out the truth before she lost her nerve.

'I'm so tired of being average, and, most of all, I'm really tired of being so scared.'

'Scared?' There was concern in his voice. 'What are you frightened of? Me?'

'This. Intimacy. Letting go of my inhibitions and simply enjoying myself with another human being.'

She squeezed her eyes shut.

'I'm not a prude or frigid. That's not the problem. I just cannot let myself relax. It's totally ridiculous. I am an adult, I'm single, and I've had more chocolate profiteroles in my life than I have had orgasms. Which for a woman of twenty-seven is a disgrace.'

Instantly she covered her mouth with her hand. 'And I have no idea why I just said that.'

'A total disgrace. You're a beautiful woman, Lottie. You deserve to be adored. Fed chocolate ice cream in bed every night. Whatever you want.'

'Thank you. But adoration is not on my list of priorities right now.'

Her hand pressed against Rob's chest. 'I am vanilla ice cream. Nice, dependable. Can be excellent. But on the whole pretty unadventurous and average.'

The rumble of a deep-seated chuckle started low in his body but when he spoke the words were murmured through the lips pressed against her forehead as he hugged her closer.

'I happen to like good vanilla dairy ice cream. There is nothing wrong with that.'

'Now you're trying to be nice to make me feel better. Please stop. It's a lot easier if you slip back into the scamp role.'

'Then let me ask you a question. How many times have

you practised a recipe in that bakery kitchen of yours before you're happy to serve it to your customers?'

Lottie laughed out loud. 'Way too many. It always takes me six or seven test batches before I have something I love.'

'Right. Same here. The only way to get past average is to test yourself in a safe environment where you are in control and no one has to see the results but you.'

'Yes, I suppose so…but where are you going with this?'

'Just this. It seems to me that the lovely Miss Rosemount needs to connect with her sensuality in a safe place where she feels comfortable and secure. With a lover who she can trust.'

'Ah, that's where you're going. And I suppose you are the perfect candidate for the position? I mean job. Role. Oh, stop laughing.'

'I can produce references and commendations should they be required.'

'Your technical prowess is not in doubt. It's the trust bit that's the killer.'

'You don't trust me?'

'I don't know you! I've met Rob Beresford the chef and I've seen Rob Beresford the TV celebrity in action everywhere I look. And this evening I got to know Rob the teenage carer. But who is Rob when the only thing that separates us is a sheet and a whiff of bakery sugar?'

'You're looking at him right now.'

Rob held his arms out wide.

'How can you not know me? You've seen me with my mother and with Sean. My family are the people that matter in my life. All of the celebrity stuff is promotion, fluff, marketing so that I can earn a living. Look at me. Really look at me.'

'What you said earlier,' Lottie asked, her voice trembling

and hesitant, 'about only being interested in the short term. Did you mean it?'

The pad of his fingertip scorched a path down from her temple to the hollow just under her ear.

'Every word. That's the way I live. No long-term relationships. No heartbreak. Just two adults who know precisely what they are getting into from the start.'

'Is that what you told Debra? Because she was heartbroken.'

Rob exhaled slowly. 'Debra thought that she could make me change my mind, that she was different and special and that my rules didn't apply to her. They did, and she didn't like it. I'm not heartless, Lottie. I was sorry that she took it badly but it worked out okay for her in the end.' His fingertips started running up and down her forearm, and every hair on her body stood to attention in response. 'And it can work out okay for you, too.'

Lottie blew out sharply and stepped back, both hands in the air, palms forwards.

'Sorry, but this is a little too much.'

His response was a knowing chuckle that rattled around inside her skull, intent on causing disruption.

'You do realise that what you are suggesting is the nearest thing to training lessons! I mean, I've read women's magazines and mix with girls who have paid professionals to help them in that area in the past. And don't scowl like that—male escorts are not unheard of. You could probably do quite well in that line of work.'

'Thanks for the compliment. I will keep that career choice in mind if I should ever fancy a change in direction.'

He shook his head slowly from side to side. 'You don't get it, gorgeous. This is a one-time offer. You're tired of being ordinary. I see the extraordinary. We're both single, consenting adults and I would seriously love to get you naked and see what happens next. There. Is that honest enough for you?'

His head tilted to one side and he turned on the killer smile that could melt ice at fifty paces. 'So come on, Lottie, take a chance on a fling. You know you want to.'

'Wait a minute. It's one thing to brainstorm an idea, but making it happen and seeing it through are a whole different matter.'

'Then I'll make it easy for you. This is Saturday night and I am going to be in town for the next three days. Three days. Three interactive lessons. I could make a start tomorrow morning if you like.'

'Tomorrow! That's fast work, cheeky. Will there be an exam at the end?'

'Oh, darling Lottie, you've already passed the exam. This is the higher education course where anything at all can happen. And I cannot wait to get started. But if you're nervous—let's say that we have an introductory taster session. On the house. Now how can you deny yourself that little treat? Tomorrow morning at the bakery. How does that sound?'

Lottie flung her hands in the air. 'Crazy! That's how it sounds. In fact—'

She never got to finish her sentence because Rob stepped in the moment she began speaking, pulled her towards him with both hands spread flat against her back, and pressed his mouth against hers. Not forcibly. She would have hit him hard if he had tried that. No, his lips and mouth moved against her lips with such exquisite gentleness that Lottie opened her mouth wider and moved into the hot moistness of that irresistible kiss.

Helpless to do anything else.

A bristly chin moved across her cheek and down into her neck.

'I can't guarantee I'll be able to keep my hands off you. You are quite irresistible, Miss Rosemount. You know that, don't you?'

She grinned, unsure of her own ability to keep her hands off *him* at that moment, but that was not good enough, and Rob lifted her chin so that he could look into her smiling eyes.

'Seriously? This is the craziest proposal that I have ever heard in my life and, believe me, after my career in banking that's saying something. So on second thoughts, I appreciate your kind offer, but...'

Before she could blink his arm wrapped around her waist, turned her towards him and Rob silenced her by pressing his mouth against hers in a kiss that was so all-encompassing, so demanding, and so very, very delicious that breathing suddenly became unimportant.

The tip of his tongue touched her tongue, sending a shock of visceral desire to parts of her body that had been very short on action for a very long time. Desire: hot, real, undeniable.

Rob pulled her even closer, deepening his intense kisses until she was light-headed enough to want him never to stop. 'All you have to do,' he whispered, his mouth closed around her upper lip, teasing and playing with it to open as he came up for air, 'is nod once for yes.'

She managed to make a gentle nod, before his head lowered and he gave her the sweetest, most loving, lingering, whispering kiss she had ever had in her life.

'Quite irresistible. But it's getting late for a couple of early birds like us.'

His hands dropped to her waist and he stepped back, giving her the time to get her breath back.

'The gallery is closed on Sundays and my mother is spending time with friends tomorrow, so how about I pop over to your place in the morning? It's going to be fun.'

He leant forward as she nodded her reply, and kissed her on the nose before grinning.

'Try not to kiss anyone else in the meantime.'

CHAPTER NINE

WHERE HAD ALL of these people come from at 11:00 a.m. on a Sunday?

Rob squeezed his way past clusters of ladies with baby buggies chatting on the pavement tables outside a branch of a well-known coffee-shop chain, but kept his head down in case they recognised him.

He had to lift his arms up high as a couple of rampaging teens hunkered low on skateboards sped down the pavement, causing chaos. Couples arm in arm, men in running gear, cyclists in bright Lycra, older men carrying newspapers, all were mingling in a typical London street with the thundering traffic only feet away.

A low chuckle bubbled up from inside Rob's chest and he smiled at an elderly lady who was looking at a book-shop window—then caught sight of him. She was clearly making the connection between the poster advertising his latest cookbook and the man strolling down the pavement next to her. Then she shook her head and shrugged. No, how ridiculous, it couldn't be.

He didn't blame her for thinking that there was no reason why Rob Beresford should be walking down a London street on a Sunday morning.

Sunday mornings were Rob's one indulgence. Downtime from the mayhem of either a Saturday night restaurant service or a night spent at some hotel or business function.

There had been a time when he would stagger home in the early hours with some gorgeous girl whose name he had written on the back of his hand using her lipstick and the light from whatever bar they had met in, but by the time he sobered up she would be gone and so would her name.

The gossip press would be surprised to know that for the past few years he had been too exhausted to do anything on a Sunday but read the trade press from the balcony of his ocean-view penthouse apartment and fuel up with coffee and bad news about the economy. Business paperwork and phone calls and emails to Beresford hotels around the world took up most of the rest of the morning before he headed out to the beach to enjoy a long late lunch with his mum.

It was a routine that worked for him. A few hours' respite before the chaos of a new week and a diary that was booked months in advance. A week in one place? Unheard of. The last time was when the Beresford Chicago was hit with a norovirus outbreak, which had closed the entire hotel right in the middle of the conference season and he'd had to drop everything to fix the problem. Not good.

So taking a full week in London in June was a very special treat. Business—of course. He had meetings in the diary with both his dad and Sean to talk about the expansion plans. But that was not the real reason. The second his mother had been invited to be the opening artist for the new gallery, he had tagged three days' holiday onto the end of his work week. Recovery time. This might be the most important exhibition of his mother's career and was certainly going to be crucial in helping her get well.

And so far it seemed to be working. It had been a long time since he had seen her so happy and content and balanced. A very long time.

This Sunday was going to be his first real day off in eighteen months.

Strange, he had never even thought about it like that until the previous evening when Sean had sent him on his way and told him to take the rest of the weekend off for a change. Give his mother a break.

A weekend off. Now that really was a strange concept.

Was that why he had looked out over the London sky-line from the penthouse apartment in the Beresford Rich-mond that morning and had only been able to think of one person that he wanted to spend it with?

Last night he had opened up to Lottie in a way that had startled him as much as it had surprised her.

He rarely talked about his past to people he had just met. Why bother? The media had done all of that for him.

But somehow Lottie had got under his skin and it mat-tered very badly that this girl understood the young man who had fought his way through catering college as a way to burn off his bitter anger and resentment so he could make good his promise to his mum.

Lottie's good opinion mattered. She was Dee's best friend, after all, and Sean was bound to let slip a lot about their life as teenagers. Yeah, that was a good plan. He could keep on telling himself that was the only reason he had blurted out his life story like a fool. Shame that was only part of the reason.

But in the middle of the night as he'd tossed and turned under his high-thread-count sheets, his mind had refused to let her go.

The image of Lottie's face as he'd kissed her whirled around into a hot dream where his fingertips explored every inch of her body from that stunning hair to the tips of those rose-painted toenails that had peeped out from her designer sandals.

So what if her vulnerability and beauty and inner strength
had reached out and grabbed him and refused to let him escape?

There was a fairy story book his mother had used to read
occasionally when he was small that told tales of beautiful half-bird-like women called sirens whose music and
singing was so irresistible and alluring that sailors jumped
overboard or crashed their ships on the rocks just to get
closer to them.

Lottie the siren, that had to be it. The girl had magical powers. It was the only logical explanation. Otherwise
things would get into seriously dodgy territory involving
a pair of green eyes that made him want to move back to
England so he could feel spring again, hair that he ached
to run his fingers through and skin so unctuously peaches
and cream he could eat it with a spoon. Or find out what it
tasted like on his tongue, more likely.

Nope. He would stick to the siren idea. That was safer.

And since resistance was futile—best go with the flow!

Rob looked up at the front of Lottie's Cake Shop and Tea
Rooms and ran a hand back through his hair.

He had not noticed that the sign was hand painted before and that the colours matched the interior decor. Stylish. Nice. Very nice.

Or the large sign that hung on a string in the half-glass
door that read: 'CLOSED'.

Lottie closed the bakery on Sundays?

Damn. He had not expected that. Not when the pavements were full of potential customers all desperate for
tea and cake. And she had mentioned baking some special
novelty cake or something today?

By cupping his hand and peering in through the glass
Rob could see that the lights were on in the kitchen, so

someone was home. He rang the doorbell and kept looking. No movement. No reply.

He had not called in advance or made a specific arrangement. What if she had company? An out-of-town relative?
A hunky rugby player of a first cousin whom she had called
in as security because she had changed her mind about their
little arrangement?

That had not been the impression he had got last night.
Far from it.

His fingers closed around his mobile phone. Sean would
know. And laugh his head off at the very thought of Rob
checking up on Lottie's family and never let him forget it.

Scratch that idea.

Glancing quickly from side to side, Rob scrolled down
his huge list of phone numbers until he found Lottie's and
pressed the button hard enough for his finger to hurt.

Phone to his ear, he rolled back his shoulders as the call
rang and rang and after a few long seconds a very croaky
and sleepy voice answered, 'Hello.'

'Good morning, Lottie. Hope I haven't woken you. *I am
here for my appointment.* Any chance you could let me in?'

There was just enough of a pause for Rob to ask, 'Lottie? Are you still there?'

He wanted to see her and tell her all the news about the
exhibition, which was already almost a sell-out, and come
up with some great ideas for a celebration party. Not have
half a conversation through a glass door and down a phone.

'Rob? Oh. Yes. Sure.' And then there was a sharp intake
of breath. 'Oh, no. I don't believe it. How stupid!' And then
the unmistakeable clatter of a phone being dropped onto
something solid.

Stupid? Who was she calling stupid? What was that all
about? He had given up his free morning to spend time with

her and she was calling him stupid? Or was there someone
else in the room with her?

Rob flipped his phone closed and pushed it deep down
inside his trouser pocket.

Either way this was a bad idea. Time to get back to ci-
vilisation.

Brow tense with frustration Rob was just turning away
when he heard the sound of a key turning in a lock and
whipped around to see Lottie peering out through a gap
in the front door.

At least he thought it was Lottie. Those startling pale
green eyes were almost grey behind the narrow slits of eyelids that seemed to be wincing at the bright sunlight bounc-
ing back from the pavement. Her lovely blonde hair was tied
back behind a stretch headband highlighting a very pale
face with a bright red circle in the centre of each cheek.
A perfect match for what looked like a pair of pink spotty
pyjamas that she was wearing under her apron.

'Rob?'

'Still here. Although I don't know why after you just
called me stupid.'

She blinked, then squeezed her eyes closed, then opened
them a little wider but winced and closed them again. 'That
wasn't you. It was me. I was the stupid one. I set the oven
timer for my cake but fell asleep.'

A quiver around her upper lip was followed by a short
gasp as she slowly turned and flung one hand in the direction of the kitchen. 'I burnt the sponges. They're completely
dried out. I never burn my cakes. And it's their golden wedding today and it's meant to be really special and I feel…
terrible. My head feels terrible.'

Then she half slumped and half collapsed onto the nearest chair. In a second her eyes fluttered closed and her head
fell forwards onto her arm, which was stretched out on the

table, so that Rob had to step inside the shop, close the door behind him and lean in closer to hear what she said next.

'I've caught your mother's rotten head cold. Everything feels fuzzy. And I think I need to have a little sleep now.'

'Oh, no, you don't,' he replied and quickly put one hand under each of her armpits and lifted her back to a seated position. 'Wake up, Lottie. Come on. You need to go and lie down for a while. Take a nap.'

She tried to shake her head but winced. 'Cake. Gloria. I need to call Gloria. Gloria can make the cake.' Then she blinked. 'Wait. That girl is hopeless at piping. I need piping.'

'Don't worry about the cake. I'll sort something out while you get your head down for half an hour.'

Lottie smiled at him. 'That sounds so good.' Then she blinked and stared at the Beresford hotel bag that he had dumped onto the table so he could pick her up.

'What's in the bag?'

'Amaretto biscuits.' He sighed and rolled his eyes. 'I thought you might like your own stash.'

'For me? That's nice. You're a nice man.'

'You wouldn't be saying that if you knew what I was thinking right now,' Rob replied through gritted teeth as he hooked one of Lottie's arms around his neck. 'Nice is not how I would describe it.'

Bright sunlight was streaming in around the side of the long roman blinds that covered the studio windows when Lottie turned over and dared open her eyes just a crack. Then a little wider.

Her head still felt as though it were stuffed with cotton and her throat was beyond scratchy but she could turn over without feeling dizzy, which was a major improvement on how she had felt earlier.

The pyjama top she was wearing had twisted into a knot under her shoulder and she wriggled into a more comfortable position in her bed and tugged the satin quilt up to her chin.

Wait a minute. She couldn't remember climbing the stairs to the loft and she certainly couldn't recall pulling the quilt from the shelf.

And just like that, fractured memories of opening the door to one of the best-known chefs on the planet came flooding back.

Groaning out loud, Lottie pushed up against the headboard and closed her eyes.

Oh, no! The one person on the planet who she did not want to see her looking like an extra from a really cheap horror movie had walked in at exactly the wrong time. He had probably run away screaming in shock.

Pressing the fingers of one hand to her forehead, she closed her eyes and tried not to picture what she must have looked like that morning after her silly attempt to make Lily's cake.

The cake!

She had to make a cake!

Blinking awake, Lottie rolled her legs over the edge of the bed and stared at her watch. Then looked again in horror. She had been asleep for hours! There was no way she had time to bake and decorate a cake before the tea party.

What was she going to do?

Run out to the supermarket and buy whatever they had left at this time on a Sunday afternoon? Or plan B, the freezer. She had cakes in the freezer. If she worked fast there might be enough time to quickly defrost a couple of sponge cakes, whip up some emergency icing and decorate with whatever she had handy. Forget the fine sugar work.

It would be tight but she might be able to manage it—if she got to work now.

Pushing her hair back from her face, Lottie stood upright, checked that she was steady. A quick splash of water on her face. A wince at the state of her hair. And she was ready for action. Sort of.

First step—find out what she could salvage in a hurry. Hopefully Rob had tossed the burnt cakes in the bin. So that left the icing.

Rob.

Had Rob really been here or had she imagined the whole thing? He had certainly played a starring role in her fevered dreams as she'd tossed and turned all night.

Yawning widely, Lottie slipped down the stairs to her kitchen, then her feet slowed.

She must have been even sicker than she had imagined because that wasn't her usual CD. Modern jazz didn't quite fit as background music for her cake shop.

She slid quietly in through the door. And froze in her stocking feet.

Rob was standing in front of the worktop.

His hands were rock steady but she could see that his gaze was totally focused and narrowed with concentration.

On the marble pastry board to one side was a panel of pale gold-coloured fondant icing that had been transformed with intricate precision into the most stunning crown of elegant and perfect edible lace that she had ever seen.

Her breath caught in her throat as he slowly and carefully lifted the fondant lace onto a sheet of baking parchment and then painstakingly placed the complete panel onto the sides of a round cake.

She dared not make a sound in case it disturbed him as he lifted away the paper. It was like watching a great artist at work.

'Behold one super-light sandwich cake. Four layers. Fresh lemon curd and pastry cream filling for the vanilla sponges at the top. My own special recipe Black Forest chocolate ganache for the two chocolate sponges on the bottom. Gold icing to cover. As ordered,' he said and stood back to check that the fondant was not moving.

'Lily prefers plain cake but Harry is a chocolate man,' she whispered through a throat that was tingling with emotion. 'It's wonderful, Rob. I love what you've done with the gold fondant. That lace design is gorgeous.'

Rob smiled back at her. 'No problem. All I did was follow the order you had pinned to the clip rail and checked the burnt cakes to make sure that you were going for two flavours. Gold lace seemed about right for a golden wedding cake. How are you feeling?'

Lottie took a few steps into the kitchen and sat down on the bar stool with her elbow on the bench.

'You mean apart from inadequate? Much better. I cannot believe that I slept for four hours. That's a first for me. But at least my headache has gone.'

'If it is my mum's cold you will be back to normal tomorrow. But in the meantime, take it easy. I've got this for you.'

'Now you're making me feel really guilty.' Lottie groaned. 'I have to do something to help.'

He walked up and down a few steps, then nodded. 'How about some gold ribbon around the pedestal? Think you can manage that? I want to finish the centrepiece before the fondant hardens up too much.'

'Got it.' She grinned and was about to slide off the stool when she blinked up at Rob, who was wiping away cornflour and icing sugar from what looked like an immaculate kitchen surface. 'What centrepiece?'

'Every wedding cake needs a centrepiece, doesn't it?

And I needed something to do while the cakes were cooling besides checking up on you.'

'You checked up on me?' Lottie blushed and self-consciously pulled the front edges of her pyjama top a little closer together.

The reply was a completely over-the-top wink. 'You snore beautifully. Has anyone ever told you that?'

'Must be my cold,' she replied and narrowed her eyes at him. 'Unfair. I'm not exactly dressed for visitors.'

'Oh, I don't know about that. You look okay to me.'

His voice was molten chocolate, which, combined with the heat going on behind those eyes, made Lottie squirm on her chair. It was the same look he had given her last night at the apartment.

How did he do it? It was as if he had an internal dial behind his eyes that went from calm, cold appraisal to steaming-hot mentally undressing in two seconds flat. And, boy, was it effective.

She was surprised that steam was not billowing out from the front of her jacket.

'Um. Cake. Let's focus on the cake. What are you doing for the…centrepiece? Oh, those are perfect.'

Lottie slid her bottom off the stool and stepped up to Rob so that she could look at the contents of the platter he had taken out of the refrigerator. She inhaled a long, slow breath and her right arm draped around the top of his jeans so that she could lean in closer.

Rob the master chef had shaped creamy gold-coloured fondant into three perfect calla lilies. The central stamen and stem were made from green crystallised angelica.

'Lilies for Lily. Why didn't I think of that?' she breathed, then held still as he laid them in a spiral pattern on the top of the icing-sugar dusting that covered the top sponge.

'One final touch. Crystallised violets. Just makes the gold pop.'

The two of them stood in silence for a second just staring at the cake with its golden crown before Lottie sniffed.

'I knew that you were good, but I had no idea how good.'

His reply was a low chuckle followed by a cheeky grin. 'Don't sound so surprised.'

But what mattered more than the words was the way his arm wrapped around her shoulder, drawing her to him, and then slid down the sleeve of her jacket, sending delicious shivers of pleasure up her arm.

He was overpowering. Too intense, too tempting.

Stupid cold. It was making her all weepy and sentimental.

He had made a cake that was far more nicely decorated than the one she had been planning. She had not asked him to do it. He simply had. Because he'd wanted to. Because he was caring and compassionate and right at that moment it was all a bit too much.

She was going to have to work extra hard to keep focused on why a fling with Rob would be a terrible idea.

The barriers between them had not gone away. Far from it. They were staring her in the face every time she looked at him.

She could do this. She could freeze him out to protect herself. She just had to.

Lottie made a dramatic gesture of checking her watch, and then slowly stepped out of the arc of his arms. 'Help! We're going to miss the tea party unless I get dressed in the next five minutes. And after all that work, you're definitely coming with me.'

Then, without thinking or hesitating, she stood on tiptoe and pressed her lips for a fraction of a second against the side of his cheek.

'Thank you for making such a beautiful cake. Lily is going to love it.'

Rob watched her shuffle back to the stairs in stunned silence, amazed by what she had just done. 'You're welcome. Any time at all.'

CHAPTER TEN

'LAUREL COURT RESIDENTIAL HOME. Second turning on the left. You can't miss it. Big stone house with a gorgeous conservatory dining room. The teas will be set up inside and then served on the lawn if the weather is warm.'

Rob flashed Lottie a quick glance from the driver's seat. 'Do you go and visit your friend very often?'

'First Sunday of the month when I can. I missed last week. Too much on with Dee being away. But Lily knows that I'll be there today.' Lottie looked at her watch and sucked in a sharp hiss. 'If we get there in time. Rotten cold. I hate being late.'

'With you on that. What? Don't give me that look. My life might be tabloid fodder but I keep my promises to people that matter. I do feel semi responsible for foisting my mother onto you in the first place, so if you want someone to blame for that cold, I am right here.'

'I can see that. Why else would I allow you to drive my precious delivery van? This is definitely a one-off in more ways than one. I'm not used to having a guest baker around the place. But it was good of you to offer to deliver the cake for me.'

Rob shuffled his bottom in the low seat and tried to get more comfortable but his gaze focused on the busy London street. He had already pushed the seat as far back as it would go but his knees almost touched the steering wheel. 'How do you drive this thing?'

Lottie laughed out loud and immediately started a coughing fit, which had her reaching for her water bottle. 'Oh, please don't make me laugh,' she replied with her hand on her throat. 'If you must know the van came from one of Dee's pals and was such a good price it was hard to turn down. It does the job. Oh. Here we are. Laurel Court. Just turn into the drive. The car park is on the left.'

Rob gritted his teeth in exasperation as he crunched the gears and slowed down to park in a narrow bay at the very end of the drive close to the house.

He sat drumming his fingers on the steering wheel for a few seconds and pushed out his lips before speaking. 'And you are sure that they know that I am just delivering the cake, right? Nothing else.'

'Absolutely.' Lottie nodded. 'I am a walking biohazard. The last thing I want is for Lily and her young-at-heart pals to go down with a twenty-four-hour head cold. Not at their age. Bad idea. It would slow them down, which is totally unacceptable. They are having far too much fun.'

Then she looked out through the windscreen and pressed her lips together. 'Too late to run away now. They've spotted the van. We would never get out of here alive if we tried to escape without delivering that cake.'

Then before Rob could protest, she rolled down the window and started waving like mad. 'Lily! We're over here. Come and meet Rob. He's my…sous-chef for the day. And he cannot wait to show you the fantastic cake he made, especially for you. Can you, Rob?'

Two hours later Lottie was driving down the side streets of London, her fingers wrapped around the steering wheel, grateful that it was late on a Sunday afternoon and the traffic was remarkably light.

Her headache was gone, her sore throat was already feeling a lot better, and the cotton wool that had clogged her brain was slowly easing away.

Which was just as well seeing as Rob was in no fit state to drive the van back to the bakery.

She slowed the van at the next set of traffic lights and grinned across at Rob, who was lying in the passenger seat with his head back and eyes closed.

'How are your toes doing? Any sign of movement yet? Or do I need to drive to the accident department?'

One eye creaked open and he slowly raised his head and glared at her. 'Did you know that they had hired a dance band? And every single lady in the place expected a samba and a foxtrot before we got to the waltzes. Even the gals with the walking frames. And forget my toes. They are so numb I wouldn't be a bit surprised if they were all broken. Oh, no, it's my rear end that got the most damage. Those gals need more medication!'

'Ah. Perhaps I should have warned you about the bottom pinchers. Don't worry. The bruising will fade away in a few days. But you have to understand, that was the best entertainment those girls have seen for a long time. Lily and her husband had the best time. You were a *total* superstar!'

'So you were watching me through the conservatory windows. I suspected as much. I hope you enjoyed the show.'

Enjoyed? Lottie had simply brought her knees up to her chest and watched in awe as this amazing man who she had only just met charmed and laughed and danced and at one point even sang along with the residents of the home as if they were old friends having a great party.

He had been remarkable. He *was* remarkable.

NINA HARRINGTON   153

But it would only make his ego swell larger if she shared just how much she had enjoyed watching him having fun and being himself.

There was no bravado or false arrogance about this version of Rob Beresford. Just the opposite.

She had been granted a glimpse of the man behind the celebrity mask and she liked what she had seen. She liked it more than was good for her.

'I did enjoy it.' She grinned. 'But to be fair I think the wine served at the special lunch may have contributed to the merriment. That stuff is pretty lethal combined with the artificial colours in the jelly and ice cream they usually have for dessert.'

'Jelly and ice cream?' Rob repeated in disbelief. 'That explains why they liked the cake so much. In fact, they demolished the cake and asked me to pass on the message that it was so nice that could you please bring more next time you visit? And more chocolate. The chocolate sponge was a hit.'

'There you go. Praise indeed. Lily knows her cakes. And there are some advantages to being so tall. At least the cake made it to the buffet table in one piece before the girls saw it. They've been making cakes all of their lives. Any supermarket factory-made baking would go straight in the bin.'

His reply was a slow shake of the head. 'Last time I faced a crowd like that was at the international bake-off challenge in Paris. It was a battle but I survived.' Then he paused and tapped one finger against his lower lip. 'Actually, that's not such a bad idea.'

'What is?' Lottie asked as she set off again.

'Beresford hotels probably have six trainee pastry chefs at any one time. Boys and girls. It would be interesting to set up a contest and ask those ladies and gentlemen to pick the winner.'

'Interesting? It would be brutal.' Then she added with a grin, 'And Lily would love it. Great idea—go for it. Although I think an idea like that is worth a small favour.'

Rob groaned out loud. 'Go on. Am I going to like this?'

'The recipe for your chocolate cake, of course—and the icing. I think that would be a fair trade. And I would hate to let the residents down after they made a special request.'

'Mmm. Not sure. That's one of my specials. I think you would have to throw in an extra incentive to make me divulge something like that,' Rob replied with a low husky tone in his voice that set the hairs on the back of Lottie's neck standing up straight.

She dared to glance quickly at his face and immediately had to calm her racing heart and focus on turning into the lane behind her bakery.

The adrenaline-pumping heat of instant attraction coursed through her veins.

This was it. If she wanted to show Rob how attracted she was to him it was now or never.

Could she do it? Could she open up her heart, let him into her life, and not regret it?

Rob made the decision for her by calmly walking around the front of the van the moment she turned off the ignition, opening the driver's door, and taking both of her hands to help her to her feet, taking her whole weight and pressing her body against his.

'How are you feeling?' he asked as his gaze drilled holes into her forehead and messed around with her brain.

'Better. Would you like to come inside for some coffee?' she managed to reply in a throat that suddenly seemed full of sand. 'Cakes on the house.'

Her reward was a smile that would defrost large ice sculptures at thirty paces. 'I've been waiting all day to hear you say those words. Lead the way.'

At catering college there had been plenty of late-night drunken clinches in dark corners of bars and sofa cuddling, but whenever it had started to get more serious she had ducked out at the last minute. Sexual stage fright. She wasn't a prude, just cautious.

To the world she was Lottie the brave, Lottie the entrepreneur, Lottie the baker. But never Lottie the woman who was afraid to show how scared and vulnerable she was.

Always putting her own sexual needs and desires into second place. Waiting until she found someone who would not trample her into the ground. Waiting for the right man to share her bed with.

Well, tonight she was determined to throw all of her common-sense caution to the wind. She turned to Rob.

She wanted this gorgeous man with his wavy dark brown hair, blue eyes, and a body that was a work of art. She wanted to feel that sexy stubble on her skin and know what it was like to be the subject of his adoration. Then seduce him right back.

Okay, so he had seen her without make-up with the head cold from Hades, but her body was not too bad and she still shaved her legs. Now and then. He wouldn't be totally repelled.

So what if he was Sean's brother and she was bound to see him again?

She liked him. More than liked him. They were adults. They could handle it, couldn't they?

A shiver ran down her back. This was going to happen; she had to make it happen. No second best. This was her selfish-indulgence and for once in her life she was going to put herself first and enjoy life to the full.

Jogging into the kitchen, Lottie flicked on the CD player and turned up the volume as the lively saxophone music filled the air.

'So you do like jazz?'

She turned to find Rob leaning on the doorjamb. Watching her swing her hips from side to side in time with the music.

'Care to dance?' he asked, and held out his hand. 'I have been in training recently.'

She glided into his arms, his hands sliding along her slender waist until they rested lightly on her hips. Instinct rather than technique or practice made her lift her arms high and cup the sides of his neck.

The music and the sensation of his hot breath on her forehead acted like a hypnotic dream where their bodies automatically knew how to move in perfect harmony.

Her heart rate and breathing moved up another notch the second her forehead dropped forward onto his chest and again he matched her, heartbeat for heartbeat, his hands tightening on her waist and holding her closer and closer by the second.

A faint smile quivered across her lips as his hands slowly slid lower until they were smoothing down the fabric of the silk shirt dress that had been in the first garment bag she had come to in the loft. Just the pressure of the slippery fabric and the heat of his fingers cupping her bottom were enough to make her catch her breath in her throat and for a second his hands stilled.

Then she broke the moment by giving a very girly giggle and pulling her head back just far enough to look at him. It meant unlocking her hands from behind his neck but it was worth it to feel the hard planes of his chest beneath her fingers.

His smiling eyes were half open and focused totally on her face, hazy with promise and desire. Any doubt she might have had that he wanted her just as much as she wanted him were instantly swept away in that one look.

Heartbeat for heartbeat. Strong and fierce and hot and sweet.

'Rob. Do you have any of that chocolate icing left? Because I have a very ticklish spot just here—' and she pointed to the corner of her mouth next to her upper lip '—which needs a large dose of licking. Think you can help with that?'

He pulled her so quickly towards him that she almost toppled over as they took one step backwards until her back pressed against the wall of her kitchen. Out of sight of the street, she did not feel exposed when one of his hands shot up to cradle the back of her head.

Trapped between the hard wall and the harder length of his body, Lottie only had time for one sharp breath before his warm, full lips crushed down onto hers in a kiss so fast and intense that breathing took second place to keeping up.

His teeth nibbled her upper lip, sending shock waves of desire and wet heat surging through her body, making her beg for more and more. It was almost unbearable when that stubble grazed her throat and started making its way down to her collarbone.

'I have wanted to do that since I first saw you in the gallery.'

In a minute that mouth would be on her breast and it would be game over for any kind of sensible thought.

The silk dress was already a crumpled wreck with the writhing, but her brain caught up with the rest of her body just long enough to realise that ripping it off here might not be such a good idea.

'I'm probably still infectious, you know,' Lottie whispered, her eyes fluttering half closed in the heady, sensuous movement of his mouth on her throat.

'How are you feeling now? There is some colour back in your cheeks.'

'A lot better. But what about you? I could be contagious. I would hate to be the reason why the mighty Rob goes down with a shocking head cold.'

'I'll take the risk. My mum gave it to me first. Generous as always.' It was more of a mumbled murmur.

Lottie's mouth went dry. She should be embarrassed. This was what she wanted, wasn't it?

'Oh, right, I see.'

'Hey. Don't look so worried. This is meant to be fun.'

'I know. It's just that I had this vision of meeting you at one of Sean and Dee's parties and having to go through the embarrassed silence and awkward first kissy thing which always make me cringe.'

'Ah. The social etiquette of the former lovers who may or may not have parted as friends. That's the advanced course, but somehow I don't think that's going to be a problem for us.'

He tapped his middle fingers several times against his forehead. 'Smart. And we get on. Right?' His grin had the power to illuminate the kitchen. *Oh, yeah, we get on.*

A shiver quivered across her back that had nothing to do with the cool evening air.

Scary thoughts flittered through her mind and she tossed her head from side to side to shake them out, blowing out in short sharp breaths.

'I don't know if I can do this. Give in to my wild side. Because, actually, I don't even know if I have a wild side.'

'Are you kidding me? You are an angel dressed to tempt any man. Smoking.'

Lottie looked down at her crumpled dress.

'It will take me five minutes to change into a mini dress. Heels. Decent underwear. You can stay there and…'

'That would make it way too obvious.' He grinned and his hands got busy on the small of her back.

'Then I have one more question. Do you have a condom in your wallet?'

That made him stop what he was doing and look at her with a wide-eyed stunned expression before his mouth relaxed into the cheekiest, sexiest grin that she had ever seen.

'I told you that I was a Boy Scout. Prepared for anything.'

'Not for this,' she replied and nipped his throat with her teeth.

And she started to unbutton his shirt. Slowly and languorously, taking her time. Prolonging the pleasure.

A summer dawn was streaming through the patio doors when Lottie turned over in the bed and reached out for Rob's warm chest, but there was nothing there.

Propping herself up on one elbow, she blinked in the early morning sunlight and scanned the room.

Rob was standing at the wide-open window, his hands loosely touching the window frame. His long, muscular legs were languid and soft compared to the tension that was only too apparent in the wide shoulder blades that were almost touching in the middle of his back. He had tugged on his boxers, which lay low on his hips, but there was no mistaking the tightness of that magnificent backside.

Lottie inhaled slowly, locking the image into her memory. No matter what happened going forwards, she was never going to forget last night and what Rob looked like at that moment.

He was so gorgeous she could have looked at him all night and it would not have been enough.

The tattoo on his arm twisted into dark eastern symbols all the way up his biceps and across his shoulder, marking him as a warrior, a man of action.

Rob Beresford had just ruined her for any other man.

Fact. And the sudden realisation made her whimper slightly at the back of her throat.

He heard her, turned his head, and smiled.

'Hey, you.'

'Hey, you back,' she whispered when her throat finally recovered.

'Sorry. I didn't mean to wake you.' His smile made the very core of her body flutter with desire and affection. 'Go back to sleep.'

'Not without you.' She grinned and waggled her eyebrows up and down a few times and then gave him a very saucy and over-the-top wink.

Rob threw back his head and laughed out loud but as her reward he padded across the wooden floorboards.

But instead of throwing himself onto her and making her morning complete, he picked up her wooden chair and dragged it closer towards the bed.

Lottie shuffled up against her wooden bedhead and brought the duvet up to cover her bare chest, which was suddenly quivering with goosebumps in the cool breeze from the wide-open window.

'Are you okay?' She yawned. 'Did something wake you up?'

'No.' He shook his head and reached out for her hand, lifting it to his lips so that he could kiss the backs of the knuckles. 'I'm fine.'

It was one of the sweetest kisses of her life and Lottie's already tender heart just popped the last little restraining band and threatened to burst out of her chest with love for this man.

'Then what is it? What do you want, Rob? What do you ache for in the middle of the night?'

He chuckled and shook his head and tried to shuffle

off the chair but Lottie tightened her grip on his hand and held fast.

'Please, talk to me. Tell me. I really do want to know.'

He hesitated and his gaze hit the floorboards for a few seconds longer than she expected, which acted like a dagger to her heart. Just when she believed that she had made a connection, the real Rob was pulling away from her and going back into that shell he had made.

'Forget it. I'm sorry. It really is none of my business,' she whispered.

'No, don't do that. Don't knock yourself down. The only reason I am reluctant to talk about it is that it had been so long since…' he exhaled slowly '…since anyone got close enough to see that there was another side to me than just the flash exterior with the drama and the shouting. It's taking a bit of getting used to.'

'I know, same here. It works both ways, remember?'

'Yeah. I remember.' He smiled and his reply came out in a hoarse whisper that she had never heard him use before.

But for once, Lottie did not say anything, just held on to his hand and smiled.

Waiting.

And he was smart enough to know precisely what she was doing and still gave her an answer.

'What do you crave, Lottie? What would give you pleasure?'

'Right now?' She wriggled down onto the soft feather duvet. 'Right now I would like to be reminded what your body feels like on my naked skin.'

His reply was a low, rough growl. 'Hold that thought, gorgeous girl.' But then his voice changed. It was serious, low, and intense. 'But I'm curious. Who do you want in your life going forwards?'

Lottie blinked, a little more awake, and shuffled higher

onto the bedhead. 'Seriously, you want to talk about this now? Oh, okay.' She covered her mouth as a huge yawn swept over her, then swallowed before trying to clear her head. 'Well, I could lie to you and tell you that after last night's crash course I want more flings. More weekends of pure selfish pleasure to make up for what I've been missing. But that would be fluff and you would see through it in a moment.'

Rob nodded, then tipped his head in a salute. 'Then tell me the truth. I can take it. What do you crave in your life? What have you always longed to have and not yet found?'

Lottie looked at his handsome face for a moment. 'What I want in my life is an ordinary man who can love me and be the last face I see every night and the first face I see every morning when I wake up. A man who will give me children and love being a father, and is prepared to woo me with such delights as a courting cake if that is what it takes. Sorry if it sounds suburban and boring and a little bit average, but there it is. That's what I truly want.'

Rob nodded twice, then exhaled slowly. 'Thank you for that. I don't often get to hear the truth. And for the record, you could never be average, no matter how much you tried. He would be a lucky man. And what the hell is a courting cake?'

'A northern tradition.' Lottie laughed. 'It used to be that the girl had to prove her skills in baking by making the man she wanted a special show-stopper of a cake, but it seems only fair to let the boys have a chance, as well.'

Lottie propped herself up on an elbow and pushed Rob's hair back over one ear with her fingertip, delighting in the pleasure it gave her that she had the right to do that.

'But what about you, Rob? What are you doing next week, next month or next year? What do you long to do with your life? You have already achieved so much.'

He inhaled through his nose and raised both arms to cup his hands beneath his head, totally relaxed, but Lottie could see that telltale crease of anxiety in his brow.

'I need to get back to my real work in the kitchens. These past few years have been a crazy roller-coaster ride, what with the TV work and helping my mum get over her issues. Spending time in London with Sean has brought it home to me just how much I miss cooking.'

Then he chuckled and gave her a wink and a grin. 'And baking. How could I forget the baking? That cake I made for Lily was fun and I meant what I said about the pastry students. Yeah, back to the kitchens I go. Grease and fish guts will be flying in all directions.'

'Ah, charming! I'll stick to my bakery, thank you.'

Then she tilted her head and smiled at him. 'You haven't answered my question, have you?'

His reply was a deep, warm laugh that reached inside her heart and found a home.

'Touché. It's actually quite simple. I want to stop feeling so guilty. I want my mother to be happy and safe and well. And most of all? Most of all I want my life back so that I can take a risk on love. And that makes me the worst and most ungrateful son in the world. But that's probably hard for you to understand—you never had to face those sorts of problems with your parents.'

CHAPTER ELEVEN

LOTTIE BLINKED AT HIM in complete disbelief and then tugged his hand until he was sitting on the bed next to her.

'Oh, Rob. I had no clue how unhappy my parents were until I started going to visit friends and their parents smiled and laughed and touched one another. Apparently that was what real families did. They hug and cuddle and talk to their children. My parents never did any of those things. Oh, Rob, they were so cold.'

She exhaled slowly.

'So I set out to make my parents happy the only way I could: By being the perfect daughter, the girl who was always top of the class, captain of the netball team, and destined for a stellar career. I killed myself working so hard night after night to get a first-class degree then the scholarship to the top management school. All so that I could take my place at my dad's investment bank and make them proud of me.

'So that was what I did, Rob. I looked the part. The right clothes and hours spent on personal grooming. All geared up to make me fit into the well-oiled machine as the newest cog in the family investment company. I felt that if I stopped being perfect, stopped working day and night for my father's approval, even for a second, then he would reject me and stop caring for me and my life would collapse in on itself.'

'What was your life like?'

'It wasn't a life. Every morning I would travel in with my dad with a smile on my face while he ignored me and read the paper, and then literally throw up in the ladies' because I hated the work so much. But ten minutes later there I would be, sitting around the boardroom table with my father watching in stony silence while I gave a faultless presentation to the bored, listless people who were earning huge sums of money to make more money. I was dying inside every second and none of them knew.'

'What happened? Why aren't you there now?'

'Two things happened in the space of twenty-four hours that changed my life. One day I was an investment banker on a clear path to being the first female CEO of the company, and the next morning—I was unemployed and alone.

'Because, you see, it turned out that I was not so perfect after all. I wasn't even who I thought I was. There was a very good reason why my dad was never satisfied with my results. Most of my life had been one long lie.'

Rob took a sharp intake of breath but stayed silent, waiting for her to finish.

'My dad had his first mini-stroke at the age of fifty-eight. He went to the company doctor that morning, complaining of really bad headaches and leg pain. He had always insisted that we ate breakfast together in deadly silence before we left the house, so he was always wolfing it down. His normal meals were stress and caffeine and the occasional cigar. He had a flight booked for a big new client in Rome a few hours later and there was always a mountain of work to do. The doctor took one look at him and wanted to call an ambulance but he said no, he was fine. Just a headache. Stubborn, you see.'

Lottie smiled and released one hand to stroke Rob's face.

'I remember begging him to go and have a check-up and he just looked at me and said, "No. This is who I am. This is what we do. Hospitals are for wimps."'

Then she shrugged.

'Two hours later he collapsed at the airport waiting for his flight. I remember rushing to the hospital, terrified. But when I got there the first thing I saw was a lovely-looking woman who I had never seen before sobbing and distraught with her arms around him. And he was grinning and kissing and hugging her and trying to reassure her. Kissing and hugging this woman. When the last time he had touched me was to shake my hand at graduation. I didn't even know that he could smile.'

There was just enough shock in Rob's eyes for her to nod in reply.

'Oh, yes. My mother arrived a few minutes later and all became clear. This woman was his mistress. And had been for the past thirty years. She was his real love, the woman who had been there all the time when he met my mother, who had the money and family connections to get him to the top. Two hours later my world was turned upside down.'

Lottie dropped her gaze onto the tattoo on Rob's arm and her fingers traced the curving blade design up and down his skin.

'My dad and his mistress were in the hospital. And my mum and I were in a taxi. We must have sat in the back of that black cab in silence for ten minutes, totally shell-shocked and frozen, trying to deal with what had just happened, I suppose. And then she started talking, really talking. And that was when she told me—for the first time—that Charles Rosemount is not my birth father.'

'What? You mean that you had no idea?'

She shook her head. 'Not a clue. Apparently my mother

had spent six months studying in Paris a couple of years after she married and fell totally in love with another student who was already married. Love at first sight, the full thing. As far as she was concerned he was the love of her life and they had a passionate affair, which lasted three months.'

'What happened? I mean, they were both married.'

'They talked about divorcing on both sides but they cared about the people who loved them and the pain the divorce would cause was just too enormous and shocking. They couldn't do it so they parted.'

'But he was the love of her life. How does that work?'

'I don't know. She only found out that she was pregnant with me a few months later and my dad was delighted. Thrilled. I was going to be the glue that held their rocky marriage together. It didn't. He hated the disruption of having a new baby in the house and his glamorous, pretty wife suddenly could not fly out to entertain business guests at a moment's notice like she had before.'

'So they stayed married, knowing that they weren't in love.'

'They stayed together because my father absolutely refused to give my mother a divorce and made it quite clear that if she even tried to leave he would be awarded custody of me and she would never see me again.'

A hard expletive exploded from Rob's mouth. 'Why? Was he so power crazed that he would use a child like that? As a pawn in some game?'

'Totally. But it was more than that. He needed the perfect family for the perfect corporate image. It looked so good on his résumé. The immaculate house, the pretty, obedient wife and clever daughter. I was always just a piece in the fake home that he built around his ego.'

'What about your real father? What do you know about him?'

'I don't know anything. She was forbidden to speak to him again so he never knew that he had a daughter. And believe me that was a long night, talking and talking. I think I did a lot of shouting, too. I don't think either of us slept much.'

Lottie's face faded. 'But the next morning, my alarm clock went off at five a.m. and I leapt out of bed the same as always so I could be ready for a six a.m. breakfast meeting. Then suddenly I sat back down again on the bed because I was dizzy and light-headed. And as I sat there with my dizzy head this wonderful feeling came over me. Because I had the craziest idea.'

She looked up into Rob's face and took his hands in hers. 'It was over. I was not going back to work in the job I hated. My dad was going to take early retirement and move to France with his lover to the house they had lived in for years. And I didn't have to impress him in exchange for a token kind word any longer. For the first time in my life, ever, I felt free. And it was as though this huge weight had been lifted away from my shoulders and I could float up in the air like a miraculous dream.'

Lottie dropped her head and when she lifted it, she could feel the tears running down her cheeks. 'I was so happy I was laughing so loudly that my mother came in to check on me. She was worried that I had totally lost it in the shock of everything that had happened. But I hadn't. It had been years since either of us had laughed and felt happy and free and joyous. I felt as though the whole world had been opened up for me. I was finally free to do what I wanted.'

'And the first person you thought of was Lily, wasn't it?' Rob replied as he wiped the tear from her cheek with his finger.

Lottie nodded. 'Yes, yes, it was. The only time that I had been truly happy was when I spent time learning to bake. That was my joy; that was my delight. Not banking.'

She knelt on the bed and squeezed his hands. 'You know the rest. I reclaimed my life and I have never been happier. Never. But here is the totally odd thing. My mother is happy, too. Happy that I have finally found something I love.'

'It isn't the same. My mother has a lot of health problems.'

'I know. But things are different now.'

Rob raised his head and those amazing blue eyes focused on her with such intensity, and burnt with an unspoken question.

'You have me. From now on we are going to look after her together. If she wants us to. But in the meantime I think it's important that I should try to catch up with my sleep before I have to start baking. If only there was some way of getting warm fast. Can you think of any ideas? Oh, yes, that will definitely do the trick. Rob!'

Rob Beresford strolled down the high street with a spring in his step. He had walked back to the Beresford Richmond for a long hot shower, shave, and a change of clothes.

But for the first time in years, the driving urge to get back to work bright and early on a Monday morning was simply not there. When he popped into Sean's office and told his PA that he was taking the day off as vacation he didn't know which of them was more shocked.

The PA or himself.

And he knew exactly who to blame for this remarkable change of heart.

The girl he had kissed goodbye that morning as she lay

half asleep and as desirable as ever in a loft studio above a bakery.

The girl he had every intention of spending the day with. If he had the stamina.

What a woman!

She had matched him in every way possible and the sex was amazing.

He might just have found his match in Lottie Rosemount. But there was one area where he knew that he had the edge: in the kitchen. Back in the hotel his chefs knew his secrets only too well. It was time to put the *B* back in the Beresford pastry chefs and he knew the perfect place to practise some cunning recipes that would put them right back at the top.

Lottie's cake shop might not be an award-winning kitchen, but it had everything he needed to have some serious fun. Starting with the girl he was going to wow with his five-star baking. She deserved the best and that was precisely what he intended to give her. Followed by a very nice dinner at a wonderful restaurant and coffee in the penthouse. And this time she would definitely be staying the night.

Rob was still chuckling along when his mobile phone rang and he absent-mindedly broke the habit of a lifetime and flicked it open without checking the caller identity.

'Rob Beresford.'

'Oh, good morning, Mr Beresford. I do hope that I have not disturbed you. This is Rupert from the Hardcastle gallery. I believe we met the other evening when Adele introduced us at the opening event for her exhibition.'

'Of course. What can I do for you?'

'Actually I was hoping to speak to Adele. She's not answering her phone and we've had a very interesting offer from a buyer for several of her pieces. Perhaps you could ask her to get in touch.'

Rob's steps slowed. 'What do you mean, get in touch?

It's almost noon. I thought that she would be there with you by now.'

'Oh, no, Mr Beresford. That's just the problem. No one has seen Adele all morning and we cannot find anyone who knows where she is. Mr Beresford?'

Too late. Rob had already cut him off and was ringing his mother's number. Which rang and rang. Same with the number for her hotel room.

Cursing, he cancelled the call and rang the numbers she had given him for her friends, who answered on the second ring.

Adele? They had not seen Adele since dinner the previous evening when they had dropped her at the hotel. They had no idea where she might be.

He stopped in the middle of the pavement, not caring that the other pedestrians had to squeeze past him.

Dread slithered through his veins.

No messages on his phone. No message for him at the hotel.

He had taken his eye off the ball and his mother had gone missing.

He had been too busy falling for Lottie that he had broken his promise to his mother to take care of her.

The worst kind of scenarios cursed through his mind and he ran one hand over his face.

Think positive. She was always forgetting to charge her phone. He knew that. But she would never just take off and not let him know.

Something was wrong. Badly wrong. And he knew just who to blame.

And he was looking at that person in his own reflection in the shop window.

Lottie Rosemount giggled for the tenth time that morning at the tin of amaretto biscuits that had been waiting for her when she eventually made it down to the kitchen almost an hour later than normal.

Rob must have sneaked them in on his way out to get changed.

What a night!

Fast, slow, then faster. Wow. That man had ruined her for any other lover, that was for sure.

Focusing on making cupcakes and a slicing cake that were even vaguely what they should be was quite a challenge, but Gloria had been a star and taken care of the breakfast customers and baked some of her emergency stock of frozen croissants, French bread and Danish pastries to keep the shelves filled.

All she had to do was make icing worth eating, decorate the cakes and then get started on the quiche and filled baguettes, and the lunch menus would be ready.

And hopefully, if she was a very good girl, Rob would come back and see her.

Now that was something to look forward to.

Grabbing a tray of cooled double-chocolate pecan-and-hazelnut brownies, Lottie strolled into the cake shop and started loading the cake stand.

And almost dropped them all.

It was Rob, but not her Rob. This was the old Rob. His face was dark and hooded with a twisted expression of anxious disappointment and anger.

What had happened? He had only been gone a couple of hours.

There was something seriously wrong.

She put down her tray and slipped off her apron to go and meet him but before she could say anything he marched past her in stony silence and headed straight for the stairs.

Running after him, with a quick shrug to Gloria, Lottie was out of breath by the time she reached the studio.

He was pacing back and forth like a caged animal, his phone pressed to one ear. Then he flung it down on the bed and tore open the patio doors, practically jumping onto the terrace.

Lottie pressed one hand to her chest and willed her heart to slow down to the point where she could speak.

'Rob, you're frightening me. What's happened? Is something wrong?'

His shoulders rolled back as though he was bracing himself to tell her some terrible news and when his voice did break the horrible silence, it was as cold and terrible as ice.

'Mum's gone missing. Not answering her phone. Nobody knows where she is. I don't even know where to start.'

Lottie coughed and took gentle hold of his arm.

'But that's not true. Adele is with Ian. He phoned less than five minutes ago to let me know that Adele is in a department-store changing room buying a new dress for a cocktail party she's been invited to. She forgot to charge her phone so he thought he had better let me know where she was. In case we were worried. Oh, Rob.'

His face twisted into relief then fury and then relief again. 'She went shopping. With Ian? Is that what you're telling me?'

Lottie smiled and held her arms out to hug him. 'She is fine. Ian met her after breakfast and they're on the way to the gallery now. Ten minutes' walk away at most.

'You can stop panicking, Rob.'

But instead of embracing her and letting her ease away his anxiety and concern, Rob turned back to the railing and his fingers clasped around the back of the patio chair so fiercely that his knuckles were almost white under the pressure.

'She is not fine. Has Ian any idea of what I've just been

through?' Each word was almost spat out into the air through his clenched teeth.

'Hey.' Lottie tried to smile but failed. 'It was good of him to be so considerate.'

'Considerate? Is that what you call it? How about calling me first? Now, that would have been considerate.'

'Well, he might have done if he had your phone number. But seeing as he didn't and Adele couldn't remember it, he phoned me instead and then was going to call the gallery to let them know they were going to be delayed. I happen to think that is very considerate.'

'Do you, indeed?' Rob nodded and blew out hard. 'Then you don't have the faintest idea what you're talking about. Because I have been down this road before.'

Then he stepped back and dropped his head. 'A few years ago my mum had planned to hold an exhibition in New York with a few friends. Private gallery, exclusive, serious pieces from some of the finest contemporary artists. She was so looking forward to it that she insisted I take time out to have a holiday with Sean and my dad and the whole extended family in the new Beresford Miami. Have a real break for once.'

A hard, low laugh shook his shoulders and Rob lifted his head and looked at Lottie. 'The gallery was broken into the night before the exhibition and they took everything. Three years' work—gone, stolen. Can you imagine how destroyed she was? Of course, I offered to try and help with the police reports and the whole mess. But no. She insisted that I leave it to the police to deal with. My family holiday was far more important.'

Rob started to pace up and down the hard wooden flooring. 'When I got back to the penthouse in New York she had moved out. Just gone, no messages, no notes. No clue as to where she was. Do you understand what that felt like?

It took me three frantic days to track her down. She had gone to the Hamptons to be alone because she didn't want anyone to see her in the dark days of a big depression that could last for weeks.'

His eyes closed for a second and when they opened again some of her Rob was back.

So that when he reached out and took her hands in his she wanted to fall into his arms and tell him that she was sorry and that it would work out if he gave them a chance.

But he whipped that moment away from her before she even opened her lips.

'I am sorry, Lottie. But this is yet another reason why it's time that we should be going. And soon.'

'Going? What do you mean "going"?'

'I need to get back to California. That's where my work is, and I'm taking my mother with me. I am so sorry, Lottie, I really am.'

Lottie folded her arms. 'California? You're leaving, just like that. Exactly who do you think you are talking to? I'm not Debra. You can't mess me around like this, Rob. It's not fair.'

He whirled around to face her with a look of total fury.

Rob stomped forward and leant towards Lottie until she could feel his hot, bitter breath on her face. 'That's where you're wrong. You're precisely the same as Debra. And don't you dare say that I didn't tell you the rules.'

She shook her head and her gaze scanned his wrecked and tragic face.

'Stay. You owe me two more lessons, remember? And don't shake your head like that. We're clever people—we can work this out.'

'I have to be the one who's walking away, before that day comes when I'm forced to decide who to put first. Because that isn't fair on either of us. I'm sorry. I truly am.'

His arms tightened, drawing her to him, and he held her there against his chest as though it was the last time they would share this precious connection.

Tears welled in her eyes at the very idea that he was walking out on her for the best reason in the world.

No, this could not be happening. Not when they had only just found one another.

It took all of her strength but she slowly pushed Rob away so that she slid out of his arms. She yearned for his touch but she knew what had to be done.

'No, Rob, no. I'm not going to let you do this to yourself. You asked me to take a chance on you. Well, now it's my turn. Change the rules. Find the love you need, right here.'

'Every time I take a chance on love it's snatched from me one way or another. That's why I need to move on before you create a hole in my heart and my soul that nothing else can fill. I'm not taking the risk, for both of our sakes.'

He instinctively stepped forwards to hold her but she pressed hard against his solid chest.

'Move on? Oh, Rob, I saw my parents waste the best years of their lives living in quiet desperation, living a lie and denying their love in case the sadness and despair seeped out between the cracks. My mother had three precious months with the love of her life before giving him up. Why? Because she was too afraid of hurting the other people in her life. And do you know what? She regretted it from the moment she got back to London. And no matter how hard she tried and how much effort she made, it did not make one bit of difference.'

Lottie caressed Rob's face with her fingertip and saw his eyelids flutter at her touch.

'That's not good enough, Rob. I want more than three months with the man I care about. I want a lifetime, and we can have that. No! Hear me out. Adele is real and honest and true. She doesn't live a lie. She never has. She is one of the bravest people that I have ever met. Just like her son. Talk to her—talk to her today.'

'Lottie, it has to be this way.'

'I don't agree. I care about you and want to be with you.'

Then she slid her hands down his chest until only her fingertips were in contact with his body.

'Go! Go and do what you have to do. But only come back to me if you are prepared to go the whole way. I feel that I've only just started to get to know the real Robert Beresford, but you need to open up and give me everything of yourself, not just the part that you want other people to see. And if you're not prepared to do that, then perhaps you should go. And not come back.'

The words caught in her throat but she managed to squeeze them out before turning to the balcony so that she did not have to see him leave in silence.

Each of his footsteps on the wooden stair drove a stake into her heart, but it was only when the kitchen door slammed shut that she finally let go of the railing and slipped back into the bedroom. That way, Rob could not see her collapsed onto the floor, overwhemed by floods of bitter tears for the empty space he had created in her life.

CHAPTER TWELVE

ROB WALKED SLOWLY through the newly refurbished Beresford Richmond dining room and mentally checked off his list of essential must-haves. Simple, clean lines blended with pale polished wood and cream-and-biscuit shades in the decor and furnishings to create a warm, welcoming ambience. No fussy red velvet or snootiness here.

His mother's connections to wonderful artists had helped the Beresford hotel group to collect a fine art collection that perfectly matched the contemporary styling.

The whole room had been created with one purpose in mind.

To allow the guests to relax and enjoy sumptuous food and wine in a comfortable and luxurious setting without old-school formality. This was all about the diners and the food.

And it worked. The awards and food-critic plaudits were flooding in.

He should be proud of what they had achieved.

Instead, his mind had been a blur of uncertainty and doubt from the minute Lottie had told him to leave.

He didn't blame her.

Rob ran one hand over his face and blinked himself awake.

Sleep had come in fits and starts and every dreaming

moment was filled with the memory of how he had held Lottie in his arms and the way her long hair flowed out onto the pillow when asleep.

Damn. He had it bad.

But he had made the right decision. For both of them.

'Hey, I thought you were heading back today.'

Sean strolled out from the kitchens with his fingers wrapped around a napkin.

'Hey yourself. I am going today. And don't get crumbs on my floor.'

Sean replied with a snort and took one last bite of the new range of savoury pastries. 'These choux buns—' he smiled between swallows '—are amazing. Three kinds of cheese. Hint of paprika. Our white-wine aficionados are going to be in heaven.'

Rob shook his head and tried to smile back but his mouth was too tight with tension as he remembered the moment that had inspired that recipe. Cheesy bites at an art gallery.

'Was that the only reason you called me down here this morning?'

'Nope, I have news. I had a very long X-rated chat with my one true love, Miss Dee Flynn, last evening, and we have finally set a date for our wedding. What are you doing last week in September—apart from being my best man?'

Rob roared with laughter and slapped Sean on the back so hard it almost sent him flying.

'That's wonderful news. Congratulations. You're a lucky man.'

'I know it. You're doing the meal. Seven-course extravaganza. Best food you ever came up with in your life, right? And you've got to have these cheese things as canapés.'

'Damn right.' Rob grinned then man-slapped Sean again. 'The best of the best, I guarantee it.'

'Ah. But it gets even better. The lovely Charlotte Rosemount is the chief bridesmaid and creator of the wedding cake.'

'Lottie is making your wedding cake? What about me?'

'Bride gets to choose. But you, my friend, have the pleasure of slow dancing with Lottie at my wedding. Now that I want to see.'

Rob sucked in a long breath, then narrowed his eyes. He remembered only too clearly what had happened the last time he danced with Lottie.

'Have I just been set up?'

'By experts,' Sean replied, and rubbed the palms of his hands together.

'This is how it works. I know Adele and Ian are more than just friends and that's great. So great that I've already told Adele that she can stay in this hotel as long as she wants.'

'No, I've got that covered,' Rob tried to interrupt but Sean stopped him.

'Not this time, matey. You're stuck with a family who does not let one of their own deal with their problems alone, especially when you're the only one around here who seems to be blind to the fact that you're walking away from one of the best things that ever happened to you.'

Sean rapped Rob hard in the centre of his forehead. 'Lottie is good for you. Deal with it.'

'Me, in a long-term relationship? That would be a first.'

'Then we have something else in common. I adore Dee and it breaks me when we are apart but I am so crazy in love with that girl that nothing in my life comes close. You deserve some of that happiness, Rob. You've kept your promise to Adele and paid in advance for some time to enjoy your life. And why are you shaking your head like that?'

'Lottie needs someone who can make her happy and love her the way she deserves. She wants one hundred per cent of who they are. That's not me. I'm like Mum, always looking for the next rush where each relationship has an expiry date. I'm not built for the long term.'

'What are you saying? That Lottie's not worth fighting for? That she's not good enough for you?'

'Don't say that. Don't you dare ever say that! She is the best woman I've ever met. If there's a problem, it's with me. Stop looking at me like that. It's freaky.'

'That's because I've never seen the mighty Rob Beresford in love before. Yes, there you go. I used the *L* word and your name in the same sentence. Actually, come to think of it, that is a little freaky. And it's certainly going to take some getting used to. But I think I am up to it.'

Sean crumpled the napkin into a ball and crushed it in his fist.

'Your call, brother. You can stay on the same track you're on now and end up as cranky old Uncle Rob to the stunningly gorgeous and talented children that Dee and I plan to produce in the near future, or, and here's a thought, you'd better grab Lottie before some other lucky man snaps her up on the rebound.'

'Lottie, you have a visitor.' Gloria rolled her eyes towards the front door and bared her teeth in a wide-mouthed scream before shaking her fingers out and blowing on the tips.

'Who is it? Not that hot bloke who wanted to join the Bake and Bitch club so that he could pick up women?'

'Well, that sounds like fun. Where do I sign up?'

Rob!

Lottie refused to turn around and give him the satisfaction of seeing her flushed face and neck. Instead she had a full-frontal view as the women gathered around the table clutched at one another, open-mouthed, and started a chain of whispers between staring at Rob in disbelief.

'Ladies, it's a huge pleasure to meet you all. Lottie has told me so much about you. I hope you don't mind but I brought along a stack of signed recipe books, which I hope you find useful. I think there should be enough for everyone. There you are. Enjoy.'

A large box slid onto the table on her left side and before she could say anything the girls flung open the lid and attacked the contents, pulling out book after book with huge squeals of glee and delight.

The next thing Lottie knew, Rob had sneaked closer and she could feel his warm breath on her neck as he whispered into her ear. 'Can you spare me five minutes? I need to talk about Dee and Sean.'

'Hello, I am running a Bake and Bitch club here. Sorry, way too busy.'

'Ladies, I'm so sorry to interrupt but I need to steal Lottie away for a short time. Ladies?'

Not one reply. The girls were having far too much fun taking photos of Rob with their smartphones and diving into the pages of the recipe book, oohing and whistling at the full-colour photographs of the baked extravaganzas.

Traitors!

'Five minutes. But that's it.'

Lottie whirled around away from the man whose very presence was making her heart sing, marched into the main part of the tea rooms, and sat down at the table closest to the entrance, her hands neatly folded in her lap.

'Five minutes. Say what you have to say, then on your way. Time starts now.'

Focusing on the pattern on the tiled floor, Lottie heard and felt Rob pull out a chair and sit down opposite her.

She desperately wanted to look at him but her mind was

too busy trying to process the tsunami of feelings that just sitting in the same room had washed over her. It staggered her that one human being could be responsible for sending her senses into such stomach-clenching, mind-reeling chaos.

'Lottie. Nice to see you again.'

'I thought you'd already left for California, so you can imagine my surprise at seeing you this evening.'

A muscular arm extended across the table towards her. It was covered in a dark grey silky fabric and she knew that the tip of the tattoo that peeked out from below the pristine pale grey shirt ended in a curving blade design across his left shoulder where her fingers had caressed his skin only a few days earlier.

And her heart broke so badly at the memory that she had to blink away the sharp sting of tears.

She wanted to hold him close and relive those precious moments in his arms and feel the heat of his mouth on hers once more before they were finally separated by thousands of miles of ocean.

Instead she had to lift her chin and pretend that she was uninterested and cool to the point of ice.

'Work. Sean needed some help at the hotel. I could have phoned and made an appointment but I had a sneaky suspicion that you would have put the phone down on me so here I am, in person, ready to take it in the chest. So fire away, Lottie. Let me have it with both barrels. Because the sooner we get this over with and start working together, the better.'

'Working together!' Lottie shot up out of her chair, fingers tented on the table, and stared at him, wide-eyed with disbelief. 'What gives you that idea?'

'Apparently my brother is marrying the magnificent Miss Dervla Flynn. I am in charge of the reception but you, my lovely, are making the wedding cake for one of the most prestigious weddings that the Beresford clan have ever seen. You and me, rocking the food. It's going to be outstanding.'

Somebody in the Bake and Bitch club laughed out loud, probably Gloria, and the sound of the London traffic echoed through the glass and made the floor shake a little. But Lottie did not hear a thing. She was way too busy trying to process what she had just heard. And failing.

'Dee wants me to make her wedding cake?' Lottie asked.

'She's ringing you tonight from Beijing.'

'Beijing. Right. Oh, my.'

Suddenly her legs felt like jelly and Lottie sat back down in her chair.

Rob pulled his chair around a little closer to hers and stretched out his arms so that his fingers were only inches from hers.

'What do you say, Lottie?' There was just enough hesitation in his voice to make her pay attention. 'Do you think you could put up with me for a few weeks while we work out how to make this wedding the best it can be?'

He tilted his head and smiled one of those sweet, heart-breaking smiles.

'Sean is important to me and I know that Dee thinks the world of you. It wouldn't surprise me in the least if you already know what kind of wedding cake she wants for her big day. Was that a nod?'

'Two stacks of individual cakes with the name of each guest piped on. Every one different and totally, totally delicious. It's going to be the most important order of my life.'

She exhaled slowly and swallowed down an egg-sized lump of emotion. 'They're really getting married?' she whispered.

Rob nodded his head up and down. Very slowly. 'They really are. According to Sean I'm his best man and you are the head bridesmaid. Full details to follow the minute she gets back.'

'Wow,' Lottie choked and lifted one hand. 'I'm going to need a moment here. And what's in that cake box?'

'I made a courting cake. For you. It's a bit of a northern tradition but I thought I would give it a twist.'

'A courting cake? You march away from me in the middle of an argument just to prove a point and then you have the nerve to turn up with a *courting* cake? What are you trying to say, Rob? That you expect me to forgive you for treating me as a poor second best when it comes to deciding where your priorities lie? Well, newsflash. I've had enough of being told what to do and what to say and being generally lied to and pushed around as though my feelings don't matter. I'm not putting up with any of that behaviour. Not any more, and especially not from you. So you can take your cake and give it to someone who has such a low opinion of herself that she's willing to put up with you. And good luck to her because she's going to need it. Goodbye and goodnight.'

'Finished yet?' he asked in a semi-serious voice.

She took a couple of breaths. 'Yes, I think so.'

'Good,' Rob replied and slid the cake box across the table in front of her. 'Because it sounds to me like you need some sugar. Try the cake. You might even like it.'

Lottie reached for the box and then whipped her hand back.

'Wait a minute. If I eat this cake it means that we are officially dating! You scoundrel! Keep that cake well away from me. No way. You heard what I said the other day.'

Rob grinned, opened up the lid, and wafted the box under Lottie's nose, pushed it even closer and then sat back in his chair.

'It's lemon drizzle.'

She pushed it back towards him. 'You cheat. That's wicked.'

'I know.' And he pushed it towards her again. 'But my mum suggested you might like it. Right after she told me in no uncertain terms that she had been taking her medication since the last painting was complete and that Ian has asked her to dinner and she has said yes. Don't look at me like that. I like him and Ian is a remarkable photographer. He would love California and my mum cannot wait to show it to him. On her own. Apparently three is a crowd.'

'Ian and Adele? Oh, I'm so pleased.' Lottie grinned and reached out to take Rob's hand and then pulled it back again. 'Are you going to sabotage them?'

'No. He cares about her. Good and bad days don't matter. I think they will be happy together. In fact, I am relying on it. You see, my mother fired me. I am now officially redundant. My services as a full-time minder are no longer required. Apparently I have looked out for her long enough and it's time for me to start enjoying myself in a totally selfish manner.'

'Wow. How are you coping with that?' Lottie whispered. And it was her Rob who grinned back in reply. 'I'm getting used to the idea that it would break her heart if I let my chance of love pass me by. Just because I'm too scared of letting a woman see me for the man that I have become.'

Tears pricked the backs of Lottie's eyes as she watched in astonishment as Rob Beresford slid off his chair and onto his knees in front of her on the floor of the cake shop.

And her heart felt as though it was going to explode with happiness.

He didn't care that the girls from the Bake and Bitch club had sneaked out and were peeking at them from behind the counter, or that a lady with a toddler in her arms was staring at them in disbelief from the back of the tea rooms.

'That's why I stayed up last night working on this recipe. Just for you, only for you. Always and for ever, my love. I know I don't deserve you, but if you give me a chance I'll show you what real love is like. Will you take a chance, Lottie? Will you take a chance on us?'

The whole room went completely silent. No one moved, not even the toddler. Lottie felt that every eye followed the movement of her hand as she slowly picked up a spoon, waved it in the air for a millisecond.

And then plunged it into the lemon drizzle courting cake, picked up a huge piece from the very centre and brought it to her lips.

Rob was smiling at her all the way as she carefully closed her mouth around the spoon and slid the moist, succulent cake onto her tongue.

An explosion of flavour made her groan out loud and her eyelids fluttered closed as she savoured every morsel. It was the most delicous thing that she had ever eaten. No way was Rob going to make this cake for any other girl. A huge round of applause and cheering burst out in the room and when she opened her eyes the first thing she saw was the expression in Rob's eyes.

And in that instant she knew what it felt like to be the most beautiful woman in the room. She was loved and loved in return.

'Good cake.' She grinned. 'You can get up now. Because my answer is yes, yes, yes.' And she fell into his arms, laughing and crying and laughing again, and knew that her heart had found the only home she would ever want.

There was a lot to be said for the perfect recipe for seduction.

* * * * *

Special Offers

Every month we put together collections and longer reads written by your favourite authors.

Here are some of next month's highlights—and don't miss our fabulous discount online!

On sale 18th April

On sale 2nd May

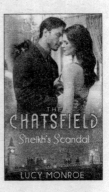

On sale 2nd May

Save 20%
on all Special Releases

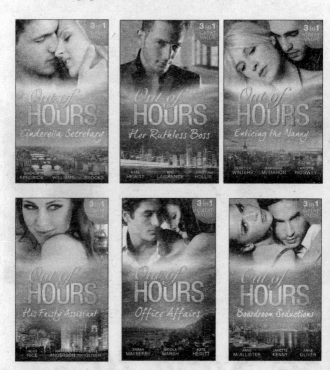

24 new stories from the leading lights of romantic fiction!

4/MB470